Gas Card

Roxanne C Fredd

Fiction

Second Edition

5-18-19

Roxanne Fredd

Also Available from Roxanne C. Fredd:

Gas Card Re-Loaded:

Addiction

If The Drugs Don't Get U The Lifestyle Will:

Additional copies maybe ordered directly from

Roxanne C. Fredd

P.O. BOX6448

Columbus, Ohio

USA

Telephone: 614-445-6131

Cover jacket design Book Layout: Roxanne C. Fredd

Copyright ©2007, by Roxanne Fredd

ISBN: 1463580053

First Print: Jan 2007

Library of Congress Cataloging-in-Publication Data

This is a work of fiction. Names, characters, places and incidents are the product of the author's imagination

Dedication To

God first in all things I do.

My parents, Gibson Sr. and Rosa Lee Coleman

To all that gave me love, support and encouragement,

"I can do all things through Christ who strengthens me."

.Philippians 4

Gas Card/Roxanne Fredd

Description of a Gas Card

Plastic key cards with small state emblem decals in particular, scale of justice, and the bale of wheat. It clearly shows that it is officially a part of thee commonwealth.

All drivers permitted the purchase of gasoline limited to fifty gallons per-week per-card. Drivers must first enter gas station to pay for the preferred gasoline. Next, insert the gas keycard into the pump, as one would do a credit card. The card may remain logged until purchase complete. This is the only way to activate a gas pump and receiving gasoline. When you have completed, remove the card depart the gas station grounds.

During this time at the gas station your life is in danger for people will and have done heartless things in hopes of acquiring Gasoline.

Gas Card/Roxanne Fredd

Description of book

The pages of this book are full of suspense, murder, love, and laughter, as you flip though you will not want to stop. This book illustrates many things that can potentially happen when people become desperate for gasoline.

The year 2024, and Mr. Smith has great need to obtain gas for his car however; without that gasoline keycard, he was not able to. Everyone in the city that owns a car wants this Keycard, however only legal drivers has received one. The gasoline prices continued to go up in the world. The State of Ohio is but one of the city's at a minuscule level. However, I question if that is the truth. On the other hand, maybe there is gas in the world and were led to believe other wise so the rich can get richer. Reality is without your ID and gas keycard, there will be no gasoline for you! "What will the people do without a gas-card? Or should I ask what will you do"?

The gas card talked about in this book is fiction

Gas Card/Roxanne Fredd

Introduction

Detective Rodney McAfee is his name. Frequently, he has appeared whenever or wherever needed. He has always believed in going out of his way to help with a worthy cause, in addition to never having lost a bad person. This time the Governor of Ohio needs help and he needs it now. Rodney McAfee will soon become head of a Gasoline Taskforce. Their job will be to find the people at the top of a gasoline conspiracy there in the State of Ohio, and stop them. Thanks to the Gasoline Taskforce, all the people in the world will know the truth about the gasoline shortage! Detective Rodney McAfee has his own team on hand, and they will answer only to him. The Governor of Ohio is whom Detective Rodney McAfee will answer to this go-round.

The year is 2024, and there is an official shortage of gasoline in America. The cost of gasoline has risen to $21.78 per gallon. Congress mandated that a keycard would be necessary to purchase gasoline.

Additionally, crime has gone up to an all time high in all cities. The city of Columbus has asked for Detective Rodney McAfee's help. Having accepted this case as a worth cause, he heads for downtown Columbus Ohio to the state building. His arrivals prolonged do to the number of ambulances that have passed. There repeated movement brings all vehicles to a standstill.

The Saint Peters Hospital in Ohio

A ten-hour work shift set for doctors, nurses, and aides at all hospitals. Patients keep arriving. The sound of ambulance sirens have been nonstop. The gasoline poisonings, combined with all the other illnesses, continued to arrive in the emergency rooms.

As the doctor pulled the white sheet over another young man's head, Nurse Jennet Blest inquired as to what his individual reflections were on today gasoline madness.

"Tell me Dr. Fredd, just how you see this gasoline madness ending. Do you think it's truly all about the need to drive? We definitely are able see how the gasoline poisonings has placed a great strain on the hospitals all over the U.S today. My God what are we to do?"

Dr. Fredd responded as he pulled off the yellow gloves, his words came out of his mouth slowly while taking steps walking toward the then closed door.

"Please set the time of death at 9:46 p.m. This man was only twenty-three years old, and now he is on his way to the overflowing morgue. He'll rest there beside scores of others who died form, stabbings or gunfights, all stupid reasons over gasoline. The morgue sets full with people who died over nothing! Damn car hijackers keep pulling people from their cars at the gas stations after they filled their car tanks! Yes, it is madness!"

Dr. Fredd continued to talk as he stepped through the jam of the now open doorway in leaving that room. His voice grows louder as he traveled down the long off-white hallway, his words echo's,

"All these young people with cars who don't have that much needed driver's licenses or keycard to get their gasoline brings on this dilemma."

The further down the hall he walked, the louder his voice became, almost shouting back to his co-worker. *"The desire to drive is too great for some people."*

The red headed nurse, Jennet Blest, whom Dr. Fredd was walking away from, left immobilized, with deep thought, as she utters softly to herself.

"I think you're right Doc. No matter what the cost to these people, they have to have gas. To me, this is all very sad. It does appear that the gas keycard has created the craziest times in the U.S ever."

A young man arriving through the E.R doors brings Nurse Jennet Blast's head about to resume her place down the hallway, to her next patient.

A young man that had peevishly worn Caucasian skin color has third- and-fourth-degree burns all over his body. The ambulance driver tells the story:

'This twenty-six-year-old was stealing gasoline from a car when the owner of the car spotted him when he looked out his back door. The owner fired his gun allowing the hot bullet to hit the gas container the young man was holding, igniting it all over him. The gas caught fire gave high flames that spread quickly all over the young man body. The gunman did call 911 for help however; by the time the fire was under control a lot of damage was done.'

ER waiting room hosted the gunman. Elderly man thinks that he came to the hospital with the police out of concern. He sits wringing his wet sweaty hands wearing a white T-shirt and puppy-dog pajamas. The gunman, clearly upset sits with his shoulders slumped over allowing his head too hung low. He rocks back and forth while he shares with the police officer seated next to him. The elderly man offers his thoughts,

"This is the fourth time I have had someone steal the gasoline right out of my car. I am tired of it, and I want it to stop."

The police officer uses his listening skills while giving a true lost for words look. As the pale looking officer, listened to the story his looks turn into a look of compassion while clearing his throat to speak out to the gunman.

'I understand your frustration, Sir. However, you cannot go shooting at people. Before this is all over, you may find yourself locked up downtown for discharging a firearm inside city limits or worse if not murder. I hope not, but it could happen.'

Doctor Lee along with Doctor Fredd labored over the young man. They tried everything to save him. But the young man died. If he had lived, what type of life could he have had? Disfigured is a difficult thing to accept and he was burnt over ninety percent of his body.

Dr. Lee used a wide tread getting from behind the curtain while shaking his head. Sadness and pain were evident on his face. Walking over to the swinging double doors, he stops in front of Officer Terry Spencer. Dr. Lee was obviously super upset as he voiced his thoughts.

"The thought of taking a piece of garden hose, putting one end into a car's gas-tank opening then sucking on the other end as if it where a drinking straw is pure insanity. How can a human being be so desperate in his attempt to obtain gasoline that he does not worry about accidently ingesting of the stuff? To have no care of the gasoline's possible ill effects on his stomach or his lungs is idiocy. If nothing else, they could have vomiting, shortness of breath, and diarrhea because of this risky behavior. We truly live in a stupid world today."

Officer Terry Spencer puts his hands on his safety belt as he responded.

"I know what you are talking about Doc. We have had so many calls come into the police satiation regarding gasoline. The callers want to know what gas poisoning can do to a person while praying the person that just stole there gas dies from it. Damn, I had to go online at home to see what the effects of gasoline are to the human body. I discovered gasoline could cause kidney disease, nerve disorders, and sudden death. I also learned that gasoline is not as absorbed by the gastrointestinal tract or the respiratory tract in adults. About twenty to fifty grams can cause severe intoxication, and three hundred fifty grams, or twelve ounces can result in death. I pray I never need to drive a car that bad."

A news report airs over the ER waiting room's television. All eyes focused on the television as the Newscaster talked,

"Congress is still considering reversing the key card mandate, more news at five." A look of disgust passed over everyone's face as the local show came back on leaving everyone in the ER waiting room to vent about the way things are in this city. Officer Terry Spencer eyes obverted back to Doctor Lee asking how that guy with the burns is doing. No words cam forth out of Doctor Lee's mouth and it would be the sadness of his eyes along with the slow closing of them that told the fact that the guy did not make it. Needing no more said, Officer Terry Spencer strolled over to his fellow officer and the gunman. Standing in front of the gunman Officer Terry Spencer requested him to rise and turn around. As the man fallowed dirictions, Officer Terry Spencer took out his cuffs and said 'You're under arrest sir'. Not a sound from the other people seated there in the waiting area, only gapping eye with questions behind them as the two officers walked the man with the puppy dog P.js out.

With all the action over a fat woman over in the far corner seated in the high top blue venal chair was the first to speak.

'When will all this gas stilling end?

How much worse can it get?"No one answered her although an old, gray-headed man turns his attention from the Television to the fat woman. His head moves slowly from side-to-side and his eyebrows twist up in a show of disappointment. Looking directly at the woman the old man begins to comment.

'My wife, Sue was robbed at gunpoint today after putting gas in her car. Sue stops at the gas station on Livingston Ave. She has had no problem before and this time everything seemed to be fine. However, after she pumped her gasoline and got back into the car to leave, two young men come alone, from God knows where. One grabs Sue by her hair through her open car window. He pulls her out of the car. The other man gets into the car from the passenger door. He jumped behind the wheel and they both take off with the car and a full tank of gas leaving Sue lying on the ground like an old dirty towel. My wife is 65 years old. She may never fully recover from this and I don't know what I will do if I lose my Sue.'

Next to talk was a young man, around thirty-five years old, with a trim haircut, also waiting in the ER, is holding his son. He cannot help but listen to the two people talking. When the room is quiet, the young man clears his throat and enters the conversation about the gasoline.

"I lost my job working at a factory making $22.93 an hour. Due to the high cost of gas and the older model vehicle I drive. I still don't make enough money to make ends meet. I have hospital bills for my son and I have my mortgage payments. You see, my son has a spinal disease. Sometimes, I can feel the pain of defeat eating away at my spirit. However, my family keeps me going. Now my family and I are having trouble fighting with public assistance. They will not give us any help because I am the head of the household and I am able to work. Several things make me angry at the system. One, I'm willing to work. Two, I have a license and keycard to get gasoline. Nevertheless, having to choose between food and gasoline is an impossible choice. To get to work I need gasoline. On the other hand, I have to feed my children and I have to have a job to feed my children. It is a vicious cycle. The people working for the State don't

21

really comprehend what is going on with people like me. They look at me as if I were a worthless bum."

The conversation abruptly ends as the sliding doors open and an ambulance team enters the hospital shouting, *"We need assistance, stat."*

Dr. Willis jumps up from the computer monitor, asking, *"What do you have coming in?"*

"We have a man beaten badly. It appears to have been a home invasion," The ambulance team leader responded.

"Mr. Butler is the vic. He told us they wanted his gas keycard. We started an IV and gave him something for his pain. His pressure started out low but it appears stabilized. He may have internal bleeding, and his left arm looks to be broken."

"We will need X-rays to reveal us the damage." The doctor replied.

Dr. Willis checks the damage to Mr. Butler's chest and instructs one of the nurses,

Call for the X-ray team to come to ER with a portable X-ray."

The doctor continues listening to Mr. Butler's chest, and then instructs the other nurse,

"Call up to surgery. Tell them to prep for a man, age forty-seven. He has internal bleeding. Be ready to crack his chest to stop the bleeding. When that portable X-ray arrives send it up to surgery too."

Dr. Fredd is talking on the phone instructing a father on how to deliver his baby. The mother's labor pains were fifteen minutes apart and had plenty of time, but they ran out of gas on the way to the hospital. The poor man had used his fifty gallons of gasoline for the week. Pains are now ten minutes apart. He is not able to get more gas until Sunday, and today is only Friday. 911 will be dispatching an ambulance when one is free. Until then, Dr. Fredd will have to direct them over the phone and get them through the birthing process. Tragic as it is, what else can he do? When will this madness end? When will the gasoline shortage end? Perhaps it will never end.

Gas Card/Roxanne Fredd

In the Governor's Office

After trying all possibilities and ways of cutting down the crime in the fine city of Columbus, Ohio Governor Andrew called Detective Rodney McAfee. He was his last approach to getting some help. The Detective did not receive the call for help half-heartedly. Only after Governor Andrew gave a generous plea did he agree to meet with him in his office.

Then after hanging up the phone from talking to Governor Andrew, Detective Rodney McAfee reaches for his abdomen. The man he just finished talking to brought about a nervous, sick feeling in the pit of his stomach. This unsettling left behind from a past occurrence between the two men and a woman. Back before Rodney McAfee became detective, and before Governor Andrew ever thought about being a governor, the two men were the best of friends called each other brother. They met in College while sharing a dorm together, graduated together, and called each other brothers by a different mother.

Rodney McAfee went off to the Army. Steven Andrew crossed the line of trust by going after Rodney's girl, that special one, Rodney's wife-to-be. Instead, she became Mrs. Steven Andrew. Detective Rodney McAfee often remembers the day he received that Dear Rodney letter from his one true love, that letter that told him of the up coming marriage to Steven. The same unset-stomach feeling hit him then. He has never forgotten or forgiven Steven for that betrayal. The true messed up part of it was he still loves Steven Andrew as a brother, he will just never trust him.

The arrival of Detective Rodney McAfee was promptly at 9:15a.m with his coffee in hand. Governor Andrew's secretary showed him into the governor's office where Governor Andrew set waiting.

Only after the detective had taken his seat did Governor Andrew utilize his left, oversized hand to rub his face, starting at his temples and slowly coming down to stop around his chin. He allowed his hand to rest on his chin, as he tried to find a way to start his plea for help. While staring Detective Rodney McAfee deep in the eye, the Governor found the man within himself allowing it to push through, Governor Andrew began,

"I know I put bad history between us back in our past. I pray we can put the past in the past and leave it there. The people of Ohio need help, and I believe you are the one man that can bring a stop to some of their problems. No one could have foreseen a gasoline shortage turning into an unfortunate gasoline drought. This special keycard required to purchase gasoline has been more trouble to the people than it has helped. Congress created that mandate in the hopes of cutting down on how much gasoline will be used. However, it has not worked out that way.

In the beginning, the governmental freeze of no new driver license until further notice took everyone by shock. That notice produced the fatal blow to younger car owners in the United States' All their dreams of driving shattered. I think you will agree with me when I say, "85 % of the young people in the United States drive before getting a valid drivers license. People were still focusing on the freeze when that call went out over all public communications to licensed drivers in the United States:

"Come to your local Department of Motor Vehicles show your valid driver's license as proof of your ID, plus a Social Security card to receive a gasoline keycard."

The people showed up to receive their Plastic keycard affixed to a leaflet. All significant information placed on the back of the leaflet, this keycard will allow only a licensed driver to purchase fifty gallon's of gas per week, placing a limit of movement on all vehicles for the week.'

Governor Andrew would have gone on talking to about the new things he can see causing problems today in 2024, except Rodney had one or two questions to ask. He made a hold-up,-stop, time-out sign with his hands. When Governor Andrew stopped talking, Detective McAfee leaned forward in his seat and questions, in his deep, manly voice,

"Tell me how the many drivers who have a license but are on suspension for a short time, will get their gas or driver's license back?"

The governor supposed,

"Hell, man! The people known to drive under the influence, knowing they're not supposed to be driving, but they do, because of their jobs."

Detective McAfee answers,

"Well, yes, I believe so."

Detective McAfee then took in a deep breath of air, letting it out slowly though his nose, before he asked,

'Illegal aliens, what about them, the ones which live here in this country how about them? How will they get gas to drive around?"

The governor struggled to stay polite, saying,

"Look, Rodney, the words coming from the government are: 'Tough luck to them all! Think of it this way, the government can limit the amount of people who are able to drive in the United States'"

Then he continues with his point before Rodney can cut back in with more questions.

"Now that every one has gone crazy with the need for gasoline, gas trucks are being hijacked, and this goes along with the use of fraudulent gas keycards in my state, as well as other things. Now gasoline is in greater demand than crack, cocaine, or sex."

The governor continued talking as his voice went up a tone,

"God knows I have done some bad things in my life that I'm not swollen with pride for, but I have tried to be a good governor for the people here in Ohio.

"Last week, I stumbled on a letter in the mail, addressed to me, with no return address, which read, 'if you like money, call this number: 445-4545. Out of curiosity, I called. The voice offered a deal to me if I put together a panel of judges and police officers to handle matters with criminals using counterfeit gas keycards In return, I will receive a handsome pay. They give me time to think. But I used that time to locate you."

Governor Andrew turns super humble as he stated,

"We need you, detective. I'm appointing you as head of a Gasoline Taskforce. You can pick the other members of your team. Your team will answer only to you, and you will answer to me."

The question put to Detective Rodney McAfee now was,

"Can you do it?"

Governor Andrew trusted that Rodney would say. Yes. Reaching out to shake hands on the agreement, Detective Rodney McAfee reaches back while stating,

"'I will do my best!"

Next, Governor Andrew hands a no limit gas key card to Detective Rodney McAfee, while smiling, offering up a joke,

"Do you think you will need this?"

Team members:

Rodney McAfee is head detective. He has worked Special Forces for the last ten years of his life. The government calls on him whenever they think they may need him to do the impossible. He and his team go undercover and clean out corrupt government offices. I never, ever tell what he looks like, but everyone knows "To know him is to love him. The other four-team members with him make a team of five.

First is Detective Anne Potter. She has nine years in the field. Anne wears her brown hair in a ponytail, she stands five-foot-four, at 137 pounds, and all muscle. She is a lady who can take care of herself.

The second and third detective come with three years in the field, and they are Gibson W. Goodwin and J. Charley Woo. The fifth person to round out the team is Booker T.

Then we have Gibson W. Goodwin. He is standing at six feet, with very mean-looking eyes. In fact, if asked "when is the last time you seen Goodwin smile?" No one in the team would nor could remember ever seeing him smile. Gibson came up having a hard time in school as a young man. As one of the minorities at Winches High School, fighting is what Gibson had to do going and coming. Because he is larger than an average boy his age, the boys would jump him. Nevertheless, he never gave up going to school. After he joined the football team in his last years of high school and helped to win a championship game, things became easier. Gibson graduated from high school with high honors. From there, he joined the US Armed Forces. This is where he and Rodney came across each other. One day, Gibson's sergeant was treating him unfairly, when Rodney happen to be coming past, overhearing the severity of the statements made to Gibson. He felt it to be racially and culturally wrong. Therefore, he stepped in as a captain and gave a written reprimand to the sergeant. Since then, Gibson *and he have been* the best of friends and have worked many cases together.

Detective Jennet Charley Woo is his name, but he only uses J. Charley Woo because of all the fighting he had to do growing up. The 'jennet' comes from his grandmother, Jennet Woo. Detective J. Charley Woo stands five foot even with bulging muscles to go with his short, platinum-blonde hair. He has a wife and three children. Sometimes, we may be out on a case for six months to a year, working to bring down the bad person. Everyone sees how hard it is on Detective J. Charley Woo; however, it has to be even harder on his family. J. Charley Woo is like a brother to Rodney. He holds a double-black belt in jujitsu. Before he and his family made the USA their home, Rodney had the opportunity of going to his country Tokyo. While there on one of many tours of military duty, Rodney saw J. Charley Woo compete for and receive his belt. He always has a smile or a joke coming out of his mouth. J. Charley Woo, along with Gibson, makes a damn good pair. Together they definitely make the good cop, bad cop profile work for them.

A fifth person, Booker T., completes the people needed for this team. His job is to collect all information for all cases, research it, check crime scenes repeatedly, and plan strategies for the teams. Booker T. is just twenty-one, with an IQ of great magnitude. When Booker T. was in high school, his grade-point average was 4.05. He is the best profiler alive. He completed his college schooling at a top university in half the average time needed to receive his bachelor's degree. He stands six foot one, wears his hair long down on his neck; he sports blue contacts to cut back on his nerdy look. Booker T. also looks excessively thin because at age nine, he went to work with his mother, a scientist. While he was there, one of the lab techs showed him what meat looks like under a microscope. After that, he became vegetarian, never eating meat again.

As the head, Rodney felt that the best approach for this case should be two teams. The governor gave him a no-limit gas keycard, plus all the information he could find out about hijacked company trucks and fake gas cards.

The governor also signed off on whatever is need to get the job done. Giving the taskforce permission to use all the force Rodney may feel is necessary. A judge appointed by the governor himself will sign all warrants if needed. If Rodney every felt the need to get into some locked door, we can kick it down. As the head detective, of this team all decisions left up to he.

The Taskforce headquarters is a large, loft apartment on the north end of town. There are large, crank-out windows on three of the walls, in addition are windows in the ceiling, pointing up like a steeple, the fourth wall is red brick along with beautiful, dark, wood, stained floors. There are four basic chairs, two folded-up beds, a computer, printer, and a fax machine, all set up on a long banquet table with two phones. On the kitchen counter, they have a coffeemaker, foam cups, and sugar. There is no stove or refrigerator.

Detectives Gibson W. Goodwin and J. Charley Woo will handle the fake gasoline keycards case. While Detectives Annie Potter and Rodney work on the case with the two hijacked gasoline tankers, taken five days apart and found empty in the Short North end of town. all the evidence points to an inside job. Our search will start at the police station in the Short North, looking through files on the hijacking and the two dead. Rodney then decided to sign the files out and take them to the base; it will be just a matter of time before we find something to move on."

Opening: Rodney is right, the team will soon find out about Mike Swirl. Life for Mike Swirl was hard. His mother and father both were on heroin. What most people would call good food was hard to find in Mike's house. As a kid going to grade school, Mike Swirl never had new clothing or shoes, unless his grandparents took him shopping, and even then, he had to leave his new things at his grandparents' house. If Mike Swirl took his new things home to his own house, his parents would sell them the same night. Mike Swirl found out at an early age how to survive. When Mike Swirl was nine years old, his mother turned up dead due to prostitution. The car had only one man in it when she got in. He pulled out from the curb, drove down the street, and stopped at a red streetlight, where two other men jumped in. She jumped in the wrong car while out on the block that day. One day, Mike Swirl overhears a person talking of the types of things done to his mom the day she died. "Betty was put though hell before she died." Learning the truth about that day left a pain that will never go away. Mike Swirl deeply wounded over the loss of his mother that he became very bitter against all people. She may not have been the best mom in the world, but she was his mommy.

This bitterness filled Mike Swirl to the point that, by twelve, he did things that no other kid would have the courage to do, the other kids, knowing the meanness he holds inside of him, dared Mike Swirl to do things like,

"Go slap that old lady in the face; that one over there at the bus stops, looking up and down the street for the bus.' For a price, he would go do anything. One time, he took two-dozens eggs to the middle school on Beck Street and flung eggs all over the teachers' front windshields. Mike Swirl never did make it to high school. When he became thirteen, he started drug dealing. One of his best customers was his father! Some nights, he could not go home, because of his dad bugging him all night for more drugs, even though he had no money to pay for it.

At age seventeen, Mike would prepare the dope to inject into the side of his dad's neck. By this time, his dad had used up all his veins all over his body and had large pus sores on his arms, legs, feet, and penis. Mike Swirl grew tired of his dad looking the way he did. Therefore, when he got his next round of dope in, he saved some for his dad. He knew his dad would love this hit, because it was pure heroin. This hit will take his dad up to see his mother. Mike Swirl took care of all his business early that day, and then he went to see his father. He prepared the hit of dope and injected it into his father's neck. Mike Swirl then gently pulled out the needle and stepped back to see what he thought would be joy on his father's face.

Not true. That viewing of his father's face as he took that last ride on that white cloud truly hurt! A hurt that gave even more pain to an already damaged little boy standing inside of man sized shoes. It took the last of Mike Swirl's emotions. He wanted to cry for his father while looking at him. He wanted to cry for his dad as he did for his mother. However, no tears would come to his eyes. All Mike had was a feeling deep inside the pit of his chest that he has lost something very dear to him. Mike Swirl decided to stop selling drugs shortly after that day. Every time he faced a junkie, he saw his father. A short time after his dad went to sleep, his grandmamma passed away. Mike Swirl still could not cry. After he stopped selling drugs, he talked to a friend about his need of money for rent. That friend dropped his name to the mob for a job killing a big mouth man who they thought had secretly talked to the FBI.

Mike really does not remember when he fell into bed with the mob, but he was the go-to man for a large price. Whenever the local mob had an important job to do, like getting a person out of the way, or if money was coming up short from someone, or if someone had not paid up, a call went out to Mike Swirl, that deadly-but-pretty, sweet-talking man who would do whatever for a price. Being the man for the mob, he was able to move into one of the houses the mob owned, living there rent-free. Now he only stops over to see his grandfather every now and then to see if he needs some help or some money. This time, Mike Swirl's orders were to get the routes of the gasoline tankers' from the secretaries of the Sun Gas and Blue Grass Gas Companies.

His job was to get information on when and where the gas trucks would travel carrying gasoline. The routes changed on every departure from each Gas Company and gas station. This put a stop to the hijackers for a short time.

Mike Swirl knew he could get the info on the new routes by using his seductive ways. Natasha Harper will become Mike Swirl's first victim. Natasha Harper was the secretary for the Sun Gas Company. She had worked for the Sun Gas Company for five long years without ever taking a vacation. Her work was her life. Before this job, Natasha spent her time helping take care of her sick mother while going to college. Natasha's father, being the minister for the community church, stopped Natasha from dating when she was younger.

As she became a grown woman, no boy or man would ask her out. If one did, most times Natasha said she had no time. Natasha's life always appeared consumed with three things (1) school, (2) caring for mother, and (3) getting her rest. Poor Natasha had never gone out on a date in her life.

One morning, while waiting for the bus, Natasha Harper saw the most gorgeous man sitting at her bus stop. She had never seen him there before. Seeing the puzzled look on Natasha's face created the window of opportunity for Mike to say,

"Hello."

She could not believe her ears when Mike spoke. She felt her body float off the ground. He introduced himself as Glen Turner, saying that he happened to be at the bus stop due to three flat tires on his new car.

Mike then asked Natasha out to dinner after the repair of his tires.

Natasha gazed into his eyes and said, "Yes," while her head was moving, saying "No."

Mike smiled and asked for her phone number. Explaining how this would allow him to call Natasha if things changed.

All day, Natasha Harper had trouble doing her work. She kept thinking of Glen, how sweet he was. After work, she raced home to her bedroom and opened up her closet door to see what she would wear. She tried on dress after dress, but she could not decide on what to wear. Then the phone rang. She started not to pick it up. Her hand reached out for the phone repeatedly, but, she continued to pull it back. She went through that for what felt like forever, and then she finally grabbed the phone.

"*Hello,*" ventured out low and very softly as she tried to talk, but her air remained stuck in her voice box.

The voice on the other side of the phone said, "*I will be on my way to your house as soon as you tell me where to come.*"

Natasha Harper told him where she lived, but she required one half hour for her to get ready. Glen gave a soft chuckle and whispered in a deep voice, "*Okay.*"

Things moved quickly from there. The first night he was a gentleman. He pushed in her chair at dinner, opened and closed her car door, then walked Natasha to her apartment door and said, "Goodnight" without trying to kiss her. The next night, he came to her door with Asian food for two, one candle, a bottle of red wine with two long-necked glasses, and a red light bulb. On that night, Natasha Harper bodily and mentally was consumed on the floor of her apartment by him. Natasha never thought she would give herself to a man without marriage. She had never felt what he gave her before in her whole life. Now, the question came to her, "Will he stay in my life forever?"

On the third night, they enjoyed each other again. Natasha became the property of Glen Turner/Mike Swirl, who gave her promises of love and happiness. After three days and two nights of blissful enjoyment with Mike Swirl, she gave up the information he needed. Too bad, she would never enjoy the promises he gave to her. The good-looking, sweet Mike Swirl never, ever left witnesses or loose ends, and Natasha was a loose end. Although he had begun to feel truly incredible feelings for this young lady named Natasha Harper, Mike knows what he has to do! It has been a long time since he has allowed himself to feel enough for anyone. The innocence of this woman made him feel as if happiness was possible. Natasha Harper lingered in front of the large patio windows. Her view of the city was breathtaking. The sunset from the ninth floor of her apartment held her action; it was at this time that Mike stepped up to her with his straight razor in his left hand! Holding the razor down at his side where she could not see it, he allowed her to feel the joy of the moment. As he began pressing his chest to her back, pulling her closer to him with tears filling his eyes, he said in his sweet, soft deep voice,

"Close your eyes."

She did as he asked, and just that quickly, it was over; he cut Natasha's throat. As her body went limp in his arms, Mike held on to her and carried Natasha to the sofa to lie her down. Mike kissed Natasha's forehead one last time as his tears dripped on her face.

Damn! How he hated himself for what he had to do, but he had a code that he lived by, no loose ends. As he left Natasha's apartment, going for his next victim, Mike swore to himself that he would never do things this way again.

The second victim worked as a secretary for a company called Blue Grass Gas. A man, named Timothy Alan, was also found dead. Detective Booker T, the profiler, had worked all night to find the correlation between the fatalities of the two secretaries. How did the killer get them to cooperate with him?

Detective Rodney McAfee arrived at the office at 7:30 a.m., coffee in hand. The sun mounting up overhead gave light through the glass ceiling, however, it still was not enough light. Therefore, he hit the lights hanging over the two-sided blackboard they used for work. This way, he was able to see clearly, both sides walking slowly around it. Detective McAfee lingered longer with the side of the board that showed the photos of the two murdered secretaries. He began to talk to him self aloud,

"What was the correlation? Both people are secretaries. Gas Company: the woman had her throat cut with a razor sharp object, then placed comfortably on the sofa. When canvassing her apartment area, several neighbors reported, 'She has been seen with a very good-looking man lately.'

The man, Timothy, has been sliced viciously over and over again in the face, forearms and hands with the same razor-sharp object showing he tried to defend himself. Timothy found left dead in his apartment on the floor. Both people working the same type of jobs, and being true homebodies. Somehow, these two individuals knew their attacker. Natasha Harper and Timothy Alan allowed this person into their homes. When they did not show up for work someone came looking for them; they never missed a day of work. Both the same, but one is a man and one a woman. Male, female, how did he get both to give up information on the route changes? Could it be? This guy is gay?

That is it!"

When the answer came clear to Detective Rodney McAfee, Detective Booker T. rose up from his sleeping place on one of the foldout beds over in the corner, and stated,

"I worked so late on this part of the case, I decided to stay overnight. I was too exhausted to drive home after reading the diary of Timothy Alan. I found it so very interesting. I had a hunch, so I went back over to Timothy Alan's apartment. There had to be more to the deceased man than meets the eye. It was not until I looked around a second time did I say to myself this guys' place is clean—almost too clean for a man. Moreover, dresser drawers held a mix of men and women's underwear, the real sexy ones for a woman. There were also dresses in the closet. However, the shoes gave it all away: They read Size 11w in the female shoe. That is a very big foot. Therefore, he has to be a cross-dresser!"

Detective Booker T. told Detective Rodney McAfee how he found something beneath the mattress of the Timothy Alan's bedroom.

A nice sized book that tells it all, dates, places, and times for when the deceased went out. There also were names in this book. "I think this may be the big break in this part of the case we needed."

Detective Booker T. moved from the bed to a seat in the office's reading chair. He began to state how he had considered calling Detective Rodney McAfee when he found out about the man/woman, but he knew he would be the first one in the office, so he waited.

"We also have pictures of the deceased man dressed in women's clothing, and a diary with names, places, and times for the week he was murdered. Timothy Alan became acquainted with a man called Glen and fell in love. They were going to go to Mexico City together on the money from the gasoline hijacking. The man named Glen was described the same way as with the girl: 'A good-looking man."

Detective Booker T looked through the diary, seeing every secret, dream, and desire of the gay man. The diary existed as Timothy Alan's best friend; the details in it showed every date the man ever had been on in his life.

Three dates in detail appeared in the diary. This person had not yet come out of the closet. Detective Booker T began to read aloud,

"It's been two days since Glen came into my life. He is so good-looking and well dressed. I can only pray that Glen is the man for me".

"Today is Tuesday. Glen and I talked on the phone, off and on all day, and I will be seeing him tomorrow."

"Oh, diary, I think I am in love."

"It was three p.m. in front of The Do-Drop that we got together. Today, he showed up fifteen minutes late, but he did call to say he would be late."

"At dinner, Glen asked me to go away to Mexico City with him on the money from the gasoline hijacking.

"Oh, diary, Glen has a plan, and I am in it. I wish he would kiss me, but he just hugs me all the time, although he gives great hugs. He smells so good whenever he touches my hand. Glen's scent lingers on me. Oh, Yes! The smell and touch of him gives me a tingle in my spine whenever we embrace.

"Whenever we say goodnight at the door of my apartment, he just hugs me, and I go numb.'

"Glen and I will meet tomorrow night here inside my apartment for a home-cooked dinner and to obtain the route on the gas trucks.

"maybe, Just maybe when he comes in, we can do a little more than just hugging."

Just then Booker T. looked up at Detective Rodney McAfee to say, "That was the last entry, but across the street from the Do-Drop, isn't there a bank?"

56

Detective McAfee responded while heading for the door stating, *"There should be a camera on the Mac machine; maybe we can get a shot of this Glen's face from there."*

Next stop for Detective Rodney McAfee's was the bank, he requested the videotapes from that time of day outside the bank. Detective McAfee's time with security, looking over the tapes, was boring. They offered him coffee after he had been there half the day and the coffee was old. Nevertheless, being top man does not mean free brownies.

After several enlargements of the photo, a face lifted. The scene was of the two men embracing for a short time. Detective Rodney McAfee could not help but smile as he said, "Got-CHA!"

Next stop was the databanks of suspect photos to come across a name match. A match came back twenty minutes later. The name was Mike Swirl, age twenty-six, and he was a good-looking man. His first run-in with the law was at age nine for breaking and entering. The list went on from drug possession to car theft. Mike Swirl had had a number of run-ins with the law. Although none of which were murder or violent crimes? His address was on the West Side: 249 Clump Street, Apartment A. The face or name from the databank did not go with the name in this diary. This could cause a problem. Detective Rodney McAfee jumped into his car headed to the given address for Mike Swirl. First he needed to stop and pick up his partner Detective Annie Potter. As she entered the vehicle, the photo of Mike Swirl passed to his partner. She paused for a moment, looking at Mike's picture. That moment turned into several minutes, Detective Annie Potter's first words to herself whispered very low,

"Damn, he is a good-looking man." Mmm, mmm... "Damn, he's a good-looking man"

she told her partner going on to detail of Mike Swirl's, jet-black hair cut short, fashionable for a gigolo, curly on top, making a girl long to run her hands through it. He has cheekbones that would made an old woman long to pinch them, along with a set of full, plump lips to kiss. He has a pair of eyes that would change the coldest heart. Detective Rodney McAfee had to interrupt her saying,

"enough please enough of that." She continued to look without out spoken word

Their arrival at the suspect's address at 249 Clump Street was quick. The building was a large apartment house. Detectives Annie Potter and Detectives Rodney McAfee entered the building hastily, the row of mailboxes gave a little help showing the Swirl's live in apartment number 12. The two Detectives wasted no time locating the apartment-door.

Both detectives cautiously positioned themselves on either side of the door, guns out, pointed up to the ceiling. Detective McAfee nodded for Potter to knock on the door. She did so. However, there was no answer. He nodded for Detective Annie Potter to knock again. Just then, the door very slowly opened. An old man stood there. Looking to be about eighty or eighty-five years old standing with the aid of two wooden sticks. The detectives asked to come in after showing their badges. He opened the door fully to allow both detectives to enter. The old man led the detectives into an average-looking, senior housing apartment with faded pictures of people who passed away long ago. The detectives asked questions about Mike as they sat down on the sofa. It too was very old and had an odd smell. The old man spoke slow and low toned when he said he had lived there in this building for the past twelve years.

"Mike was my grandson, although no one has seen him in the past seven years. Not since I interrupted Mike helping himself to my rent money one morning."

Mr. Swirl continued, *"I gave him a choice... "I told him if he needed money that bad, to take it, but never come back to this house." Mike decided to never come back."*

So says the old man *'Right, and I am the president of this great country.'* Detective Rodney McAfee whispered to himself as they made their way out of the building onto the street. Detective Annie Potter spoke up and said, *"I just found it hard to believe that the old man has been making it in life without help. Nevertheless, a black-and-white surveillance team would not hurt."*

'Now starts the part I love," stated Detective Rodney McAfee:

"Canvassing the area! No one ever has any answers to a police question, not until we get nasty and start smacking a person all about their head. Then the true answers often come out of them."

Detective Annie Potter and Detective Rodney McAfee walked around for a long time, asking people if they knew of Mike Swirl as they showed the photo of him. The answer was the same all over,

"No."

At the Mom and Pop store, the answer came,

"Yes, I know him."

"When was the last time you've saw him?"

"Not for a long time!"

There where five old ladies sitting out on the front of a house. The detectives showed the photo of Mike. The answers from three of them,

"No, haven't seen him! Not for a long time."

However, two of the ladies said, *"The name for that face is Glen, not Mike."*

As the detectives walked away, the old ladies went into a debate over the name of the man in the photo. The two detectives walked the streets, asking the same questions. The answers were always the same. The name was Mike or Glen, and no one had seen him lately. Detectives McAfee and Potter found themselves in the back of the grandfathers' apartment house. Sitting there were two large dumpsters, half-full. The thought of going through the trash dumpsters came into conversation. *"What you thank miss lady, you take one and I take one and see what we can find on this guy mike."* There was one dumpster per person.

Detective McAfee started to curse the person who came up with the thought that some evidence might be in the trash dump. Then he jumped into the dumpster. The smell was the most nauseating. Everything from fish heads to dog shit was in there with him. McAfee's voice repeated low

"Why am I doing this?"

Detective Annie Potter never said a word. However, her dumpster was no better. She tore open one trash bag, the odor almost made her vomit. One bag was full of Pampers, a lot of poopy baby Pampers, along with leftovers from the refrigerator. They continued to look in spite of the odor.

Several kids approach down the alleyway, headed home from school, and stopped to look at the detectives working hard, looking for evidence. Although to the children, it appeared they were looking for food. All of them laughed aloud as they ran on down the alleyway.

Then a man appeared from the door of the housing apartment. He felt sorry for the two detectives and set his trash bag over to the side. Detectives Rodney McAfee and Annie Potter continued to search as the day went on.

TEAM TWO

The fake keycards

The second team was set to work on counterfeit gas keycards. These cards are circulating throughout the city of Columbus. The fake cards have no detectable difference to the naked eye. The forged gas keycard appeared real, but the real ones hold a government decal in the lower right-hand corner that seen only under a special light inside a machine located inside all gas stations. The keycard machines linked to the gas-pumping systems. In order for a person to have a transaction pumping gas, he or she must use their gas keycard and pay for the gas. The full process was frustrating to the customer, who has to wait in line to get up to the gas pump, then leave their car to go inside the station and then wait in an even longer line inside building. They must show their keycard and pay for the gasoline.

The two Detectives pulled up into the gas station on High Street. Detective Gibson shouted,

"My God, the lines are so damn-blasted long inside and outside this station."

Both Detectives went inside to talk to the manager about the fake cards he turned in to the police. Detective J. Charley Woo found it funny to watch someone overdrawn on the gas card. Then the counter attendants taking and using their gas keycard in the Machine that would show how much was available on a twelve-inch monitor screen that faced the customers. At that moment, it was the funniest, seeing the upset person shouting,

"I got more gas on my keycard! I never got my whole 50g of gas this week, Try it one more time please. Your thing is wrong! I got more gas on my card I know I do!"

The look on the attendant face as that attendant sighs with unabashed frustration. The other customers' stood in line with faces of hopelessness. That doomed look that gave an expression revealing the inner fear that it might happen to one of them when it was their turn to use their card!

Detective J. Charley Woo shook his head as he made the statement aloud to his partner.

"This has to be how it is across the U.S. Long lines, anger, frustration, bewilderment something has got to be do ne about this and soo."

Every now and then, a fake or stolen gas keycard shows up. If detected, a button will be pushed to alert the law. The last fake card was on North High Street, In addition, to the two empty gas trucks. That is why the taskforce set up a base in the short north. Where did then imitation keycards come from? This was what our teams must find out.

Both Detective were back at the office looking at photos of people apprehended for using fake keycards. As they, worked, Detective Woo began to share his thoughts.

"I think when this case is over I'm going to take the wife and kids to Disneyland for two weeks of fun something nice for the whole family to do. I have been gone so much lately, I owe that to them."

Detective Gibson agreed to the much needed rest time when they received a phone call from the FBI.

The person on the phone said, *"Hello, my name is Agent Flip, and I understand you are working on the counterfeit gas mandate keycards?"*

Detective Gibson, holding the phone, told who he was then answered, *"Yes, we are working that case."*

The FBI Agent said, *"Well, we have two people in our holding cells that may be connected to your case. Do you want to talk to them before we ship them out?"*

"Hell, yes! Where are they being held?"

After receiving the info Detective Gibson shouted, *"Woo, let's go! The detective angels are shining down on us today."*

Both Detectives Gibson and Woo arrived at FBI headquarters. Agent Flip showed them to a room with a table and two chairs. Each detective sat in a chair while the agent sat on the end of the table. Agent Flip talked about surveillance on a place for three months. They started out looking for counterfeit money, but it changed to counterfeit gasoline keycards. There was a lot of activity going on that week, with people coming and going. The FBI busted in on the counterfeit print shop and took down the Printer and his press. *"We checked the number count on the press, and there were five hundred cards gone or sold.*

Sorry but we really do not know who made the purchases. However, it had to be someone before we came busting into the shop we have photo of every one coming and going and your welcome to a copy of them. So, now it is up to your taskforce to stop the resell of the five hundred cards, or find out the 'Who, What, When, and How' the owners are going to move them."

Detective Woo and Gibson followed Agent Flip out the door, down the along hall, to the elevator. The detectives, along with Agent Flip, went down several floors before the elevator stopped. When the doors opened, the two detectives saw a long, wide hall with cell doors on each side. As the detectives walked down the hall, they saw people inside the cells from yesterday's round up. Agent Flip opened a door; the room appeared to be an interrogation room, with a wooden table, one chair, and one-way mirror. The detectives went over to the one-way mirror. There, they gawked at the occupant in the next interrogation room. Detective Gibson read the rap sheet that Agent Flip handed him aloud.

"Name: Caskey, Tom P.; Age 69"

Caskey looked to be only fifty-five years old as he sat still at the table. He held fifteen charges under his name, but only nine convections, two probations, and different amounts of time served in different prisons. He'd been a Printer all his life.

The detectives looked at the Printer from their side of the one-way mirror as Agent Flip talked. *"He has been a Printer for the mob for years now. Because of our surveillance, we connected him to the making of counterfeit gas keycards. You ready to talk to the prisoner?"* questioned Agent Flip.

Detective J. Charley Woo answered, *"Were ready."*

The two detectives walked out of one door and into the next room. As they entered the door, Detective Gibson looked at the old man sitting in the chair, staring at the large mirror on the wall. He could not help but feel sorry for the old guy going into prison at his age. He would surely die in there, alone. The two detectives started right in with the good cop/bad cop game. One spoke with passion and niceness in his voice, while the other detective was being demanding with a harsh tone.

"I hope you're ready to die in prison this time," Detective Gibson asked the old man, although the old man did not respond.

"Can I get you something to drink?" asked Detective Woo, but the old man still in no way looked away from the mirror he was watching. *"Look, if you help us, we can help you,"* stated Detective Woo.

The old man began to glance at both detectives, who were standing at opposite ends of the table. He spoke slowly, with a slight grin on his old face. *"How you all doing tonight?"*

Detective Woo know that that was the old mans way of saying, "*I am not scared of you boys.*"

Then Mr. Caskey came right out and said what he was thinking,

"*I know I'm holding something you boys need; and believe me when I say, you boys got something this old man needs.*"

Just then, Agent Flip, who had been watching from the next room rushed over and knocked on the door as he entered.

"*Pardon me, can I talk to the two of you for a moment, please?*"

They all stepped out into the hall; leaving the old man behind in the room, Agent Flip shut the door behind them softly. Then, in a very low voice, Agent Flip said,

"*Tell me you're not thinking of making a deal with this guy?*"

He endeavored to look into Detective Woo's and Detective Gibson's eyes to see if they were telling a lie as they both shook their heads declaring, "*No, hell no.*"

Agent Flip said, '*Wright*' as he turned away from them. The two detectives, who were now standing in the hall, talking about calling their boss In order to cut a deal,. They would have to talk to Detective Rodney McAfee.

Back at the apartment bldg

Where

Mike Swirl grandfather

A melody starts to play inside the dumpster with Detective Rodney McAfee it was a tune playing on his cell phone. He began to whisper low to himself, *"Now ain't this the worst possible time for a call to come in on my phone? No way as, head detective of the Gas Card Taskforce, I should be standing inside a trash dumpster belonging to the grandfather of Mike Swirl, yes, he is my top suspect in this case for the moment. Nevertheless, here I am going though the trash for evidence. Crapper! Man! I do not know what I did, but the detective angels must be upset with me today."*

All that came across Rodney's mind and on out through his lips as he pushed a bag of trash over. Having had enough of that stench he shouted out to his partner,

"Come on, Annie, this trash dumpster thing is going nowhere for me. I am done, through, out of here."

His phone in his pocket was ringing nonstop, but he did not answer until after he got out of the dumpster and wiped off his hands with a towel from inside his car.

No-soon then the word, *"Hello"* came from *Detective* McAfee month did he hear the words,

"Hi, Rodney, it's me Gibson. Look we are at the FBI headquarters talking to the Printer of them gas keycards. The Printer may want to ask for a deal, so what do you say?

Detective McAfee hasty response to Gibson's words was, *"what type of deal was he asking for?'*

Having not got that from the Printer Gibson had to say he was not sure yet. That left Rodney to say, *"Check it out and then call me back after you find out." Rodney then hung up his phone before he shouted*

"Come on, Annie its time to go!" she did not move fast enough so he shouted. *"I think it's time we go kicking on doors."*

That really meant going barhopping for answers. Just when Detective Annie was about to drop the handful of papers she was holding in her hands, a name on a letter inside of a sealed envelope took hold of her eyes. The little window in front of the envelope read "Mike Swirl, 152 East Long Street."

Detective Annie felt good about all her hard work. She passed the envelope off to Detective Rodney McAfee until she could jump out of the dumpster. He unfastened the smudged envelope and took out the letter. After looking over the whole letter, he said, *"It's a doctor's bill."*

All Detective Rodney McAfee could do was smile at how well Mike Swirl's grandfather had lied to him. He then speculated to his co-worker while entering his car,

"I should run that old man in for that lie he told us."

As Detectives Annie waved the letter in the air both detectives began to laugh about the look on some of the faces that came past as they looked through the trash. Then she asked,

"Now, can you see why someone came up with looking in the trash?"

On the way over to check out the address on the letter, they talked about the case and how it might go higher than this Mike Swirl guy. Detective Annie Potter voiced her thoughts that this has a good possibility of the mob being somewhere in this thing. Detective Rodney McAfee's phone began to ring again. It was Detective Gibson, stating how he received a call from the FBI giving them the chance to meet the forger on the gas keycards. "Detective Woo and I had a little talk with this man. There is a possible deal out on the table. The Printer has names and places for the gasoline keycards where the plates came from, and who has your gasoline from the tankers." Detective Gibson then lowered his voice, almost whispering,

"This thing is bigger than the mob."

The phone line went silent for a moment.

"McAfee, McAfee! You still there?" asked Detective Gibson,

"Hell yes, I'm here! Damn! Man that news was so exciting, I had to pull over. Okay, Detective Gibson, tell me what the Printer need from us."

Detective Gibson then said, *"Safety protection for the girl and himself."*

"What girl! What girl are you talking about?" asked Detective Rodney McAfee. Detective Gibson informs him about the girl,

"Angie."

Then Detective Rodney McAfee remembered his daytime minutes on his cell phone.

This call was costing him money. He suggested to Detective Gibson that he hold onto that thought until their group meeting back at the base office.

"There we can talk at length."

Everyone arrived at the base office about the same time. Detective Woo had the rundown on the girl: "Angie Gooden, age twenty-two. She was new to the forgery game. I guess you could say it was her apprenticeship training. She had a long list of prostitution charges one conviction in prostitution, two drug-possession charges and all she ever did was probation."

Detective Woo began to describe her, "*She looks like she is thirteen, with her hair up in two ponytails and little girl bang cut across her forehead. She is wearing a rock band T-shirt, a pair of Capri pants, and her shoes are sandals with strings that twisted up her long legs. She shed tears the whole time Detective Gibson and I talked to her.*"

Detective Gibson said, to Detective Rodney McAfee, "*Okay, the deal is for the girl and the Printer; a safe place to live with no prosecutions and witness protection.*"

Detective Rodney McAfee thought about it and said, *"Well, if he can deliver what he says, he will need a very big rock to hide under."*

After hearing how much the Printer had to offer, Detective Rodney McAfee decided to go down to the FBI building on Front Street to meet with the Printer personally.

To agree to this deal, he did not have to talk to the governor. He arrived at the FBI at 4:30 p.m. Detective Woo called ahead to have Agent Flip meet McAfee at the front-entrance door of the FBI building. Together they went down the hall to the elevator. Agent Flip pushed the button for a lower floor. As they traveled, Detective McAfee talked to Agent Flip concerning how deep this case might go, leading to possible government conspiracies and if it did, "Can he count on Agent Flips help here within the FBI?" Agent Flip answer,

"Sure what ever I can do just call me"

McAfee then went on, saying he understood the Printer was in the custody of the FBI first, but the Gas Taskforce needed him for their case.

Agent Flip said, *"How about waiting to see what he has to say, then I'll decide."*

By this time the two of them are standing in front of one of the interrogation room doors, McAfee then asked Agent Flip to put both the Printer and Angie into one room. There he could see them interact together. Detective McAfee went into one room with the glass mirror on the wall. This allowed him to see though into the other room next door. Then Agent Flip brought Angie and Mr. Caskey, the Printer, into the room. Detective Rodney McAfee was able to see the love they had for each other. Mr. Caskey held Angie in his arms and kissed her forehead lightly. Mr. Caskey had adopted Angie as the child he never had and she had a father that did not see her as a hot piece of meat. After a moment of watching them, together, Detective McAfee was prepared to cut him a deal.

Agent Flip and Detective McAfee entered the interrogation room where the Printer still held Angie in his arms. Agent Flip introduced the head of the Gasoline Taskforce. Detective McAfee nodded his head and began to talk to Mr. Caskey, giving a confirmation on the deal, but first he need to know from Mr. Caskey how high up this would go.

The Printer's response was,

"I'm unsure. I have seen the mayor of this town leaving Mr. Big's home two times, looking peculiar or you may say strange, for lack of a better word! I also know the engraved plates for the press to make gas cards came from a U.S. Senator."

At that point, Agent Flip and Detective McAfee locked eyes with each other. Agent Flip made a gesture to McAfee with his head and hand to come out of the room. He stopped Mr. Caskey from his next words with the "stop" hand signal, telling him to hold on for a moment as the two law officers left the room. Once they were in the hall,

Agent Flip requested, in a stern but low voice to Detective Rodney McAfee,

"I'm working on this case with you and your team." Then Agent Flip voice took on a more humble tone as he said, *"Please let me become a part of the team."*

McAfee looked at Agent Flip with that *"I do not care"* look on his face and answered, *"Okay with me, Agent Flip. How about you talk to your commander, first?"*

Flip looked at Detective Rodney McAfee deep into his eyes and said in a low voice, *"I think the fewer people that know about this case, the better the chances of us living though it. I don't know about you, but I would like to live past this case."*

At the acknowledgment of Agent Flip being right, Detective Rodney McAfee took in a deep breath of concern and let go of all his cockiness. One of the first things Detective Rodney McAfee learned in Detective School 101 was that cockiness is one thing that would get an officer in this type of work killed fast. Agent Flip and Detective McAfee continued to talk. As they did so, McAfee decided to move Mr. Caskey and Angie to the base office. There, they could all stay together as Mr. Caskey provided information to help the case move along faster. Detective McAfee drove alone while Agent Flip transported the two prisoners to the base office address Detective McAfee gave him.

By now, it was after 7:00 p.m., so Detective Rodney McAfee put a call into Booker T., using his cell phone.

"Booker T., we need three more beds in addition to a stove, a refrigerator, and more chairs, along with some food, ASAP."

Detective McAfee also told Detective Booker T. about having this bad smell in his nose all day. *"I just cannot shake my overpowering feeling to go home for a quick shower and a fast change of clothing may help."*

Detective Booker T. gave the reply, *"I don't know, but I'm sure it won't hurt you. The smell could be coming from the dumpster dive you took today."*

Detective McAfee laughed.

"Okay, you got the joke."

"But you may be right."

"Oh, well."

"See you in two hours. Just let everyone know I will be there as soon as possible."

Detective Rodney McAfee hung up his phone with a closing thought to him self: *"The Printer can tell everyone what he told me later when I get there."*

Back at the base, Agent Flip arrived with Angie and Mr. Caskey. All the other detectives were there. Detective Annie Potter, having had her bath and change of clothes, amused herself by throwing darts alone. Detective Woo, along with Detective Gibson W. Goodwin, sat at their desks, working on files. Detective Booker T had his face dug into the computer monitor, working on papers that needed to become reports for the case folders they were working on. They all introduce themselves before Detective McAfee arrived.

Upon Detective Rodney McAfee's arrival, everyone sat in a circle around the blackboard. At the suggestion of Detective McAfee, Detective Annie sat on the side of the murders, and Detectives Gibson and Woo sat on the other side. Agent Flip and their two guests sat on the ends.

Detective McAfee walked around the board, pointing at different things that became clearer. Things were matching up now, thanks to the evidence the team had, plus the information coming from Mr. Caskey.

With the conformation of the identity of Mike Swirl, AKA Mr. Glen Turner, they were now able to go to work on him.

Detective McAfee passed around a photo of Mike Swirl to allow everyone to see what this good-looking man looked like. "T*hanks to Mr. Caskey, we now have an address to track down the five hundred gas keycards to Mr. Big's house. Mike Swirl prearranged the cards to be delivered to Mr. Big himself.*"

Detective Rodney McAfee felt good about the progress the team was having. He then stated, "*Now we can start to close the doors of the madhouse as we move in the direction of what I hope is the end of this case.*"

Booker T. stood with his back against the wall, facing the group of people. He tried his best to give his full attention, but he could not. There is a goddess in the room, and he is falling in love fast. Her hair and movement of her breast as she walked through the room. As time went on Booker T.'s work began to suffer, because he could not fully focus. Moreover, it was the same for Angie looking at Booker T sitting at the computer working. There was that something about Booker T. that gave her a fuzzy feeling inside her gut. She never in life had she felt this feeling for any other man and there had been a lot. The energy between the two young people is hot. Some late nights when everyone else slept Angie and Booker T. sat up talking about their past life, hopes, and dreams for the future. Once or twice, it took all they had in then not to jump each other's bones. It did not take long before everyone could see the love/lust between Angie and Booker T. coming to life.

Detective McAfee took Booker T. to the side and said, *"I'm not your father, and I'm not trying to tell you what to do. With Angie going into hiding this can't work out, Think about it man, Snap out of it, play the record all the way out. Do not let your little head back you into a corner your big head can't get you out of today. Next, think about the type of work that you do. If your work does not improve, you're out of here. I cannot use you like this. Think about it."*

It was hard, but Booker T talked to Angie about how important this case was, and when it is over, things would be different. Booker T. then took Angie into his arms and kissed her with the most passionate kiss, hoping it would hold him and her until this whole thing is over.

Gas Card/Roxanne Fredd

Cabin up in the Hills

Detective Rodney McAfee was a man of his word! That meant he would die trying to keep the Printer safe from harm. He thought about it hard. Where would be the safest place? He knew one place, his cabin up in the hills that his cousin had left to hem in his will. Just maybe the best place for them to stay. McAfee had not been there for a long time, maybe four years back. However, he still knew how to get there. Detective McAfee stopped at the all-night market to buy food to last two months.

Next, he called by cell phone to get them prepared to go. Then he came to pick up the Printer, Mr. Caskey and Angie.

He pulled up and blew his horn; the two of them came out and got in the car. Then it pulled off. Their ride there was one and a half hours up into the Ohio hills. After their arrival, Detective McAfee hung around for a short time making sure everyone would be comfortable staying there at the cabin. He then started on his way back to the base. As he traveled, a prayer came to his mind. *"Please, God, for once in their life, let them try to enjoy life. I hope that after Angie cleans the cabin, she will do some gardening or baking while Mr. Caskey is doing some fishing."*

Detective McAfee gave Mr. Caskey a cell phone with an untraceable account. before, he spent one and a half hours driving with many thoughts going through his head as he headed back to the city. The sad thing about a secret was if two people knew we all knew. Detective Rodney McAfee had no way of knowing the cell phone he left Mr. Caskey was being used to continue a deep love between Detective Booker T and Angie.

Annie and McAfee

Have a Good-looking Man to Go See

Detective McAfee told Detective Woo that he would like for him and Gibson to put a plan together that would allow the two of them to go after the five hundred gas cards. *"Detective Annie and I have a good-looking man to go see. Everyone else sits still."* Detective Rodney McAfee, along with Detective Annie Potter, left for Mike Swirl's place: #152 East Long Street. Detective McAfee felt the need to check the surroundings out first. They parked two car-lengths down on the opposite side of the street from were the house should be. The neighborhood was quiet. Not a lot of people were walking around. Then Detective Rodney McAfee spotted the large, brown door, #152, with a large knocker, shaped like a lioness head, mounted on it. Both detectives proceeded from the car to the steps;

Their hands went to the snap on their holsters. The detectives unsnapped their guns, but did not pull them out. While keeping a hand on the gun butt, they went up to the door. Standing on opposite sides, Detective McAfee knocked this time. There is no answer. He wasted no time knocking again. Mr. Mike Swirl is not home. They then stood there for a moment, looking around the up and down the street checking the vicinity, in the hope of seeing him walking up. Detective McAfee spotted a bar on the corner of an alley across the street. He made a suggestion to go over to the bar to ask questions about Swirl as he walked down the steps.

Detective Annie Potter nodded,

"Okay." As she followed him, they strapped their guns down and strolled slowly across the street.

Detective McAfee looked at the small amount of people walking up and down the street, not going into the bar on the corner of the alleyway. He wondered what type of place it would be.

Arriving to the door of the bar, both detectives stepped inside. It appeared to be a basic neighborhood bar or pub with the smell of beer and Pine Sol. There was one customer located at the bar, a drunken man sitting at the corner of the bar by the door. Detective Annie stopped at the drunk to show him the photo of Mike Swirl. Detective McAfee walked deeper into the bar with the hope of being spoken to politely by the barkeeper, who was standing at the end of the bar counter, looking at TV. Detective McAfee showed his shield, and then gave his name. Next, he pulled out the photo of Mike Swirl. He lifted his hand to show the photo when a door opened to the left of the counter and a man walked out, looking down at his gray alligator belt that matched his gray alligator shoes.

All of Mike Swirl's attention was on putting his belt straight as he took three steps forward. Feeling confident his belt was straight, he looked up. Mike Swirl saw the two detectives and the detectives saw him. From there, the chase was on.

Swirl took off though an open door to the right that led into a back office room with an exit.

Detective McAfee was sure sweet Mike Swirl had done this run repeatedly inside his head before. He was sort of getting ready, preparing himself, for the day the law would come for him. Nevertheless, he went in though the office door, jumped up, stepping on the desk as he ran across the room to the exit door. Detective Annie Potter went out the front door, running around to the alley entrance with her gun out. Detective McAfee followed though the office door into the room on Mike's heels. Detective McAfee ran around the desk right behind Mike Swirl. He never lost sight of Mike Swirl as he went out the exit door.

Now there is a thing called Murphy's Law that states, "Whatever can go wrong will go wrong." Hence, Mike Swirl just happened to be in the wrong place at the wrong time. He also went the wrong way coming out of the exit door. If sweet Mike Swirl had turned left coming out the exit door, he would have be on his way to the open end of the alley, even though Detective Annie Potter was coming down to meet him.

A turn to the right led to the dead end of the alley, a large red brick wall. Detective Rodney McAfee came out the exit door right behind Mike Swirl, who was under the brightly lit streetlight, jumping all around, frantically trying to think what to do next. Detective McAfee came to a dead stop coming out the door, but stepped up closer to see the weapon in Mike's hand. Mike Swirl had pulled his straight razor out. Detective McAfee stopped all movement forward to confront Mike Swirl. He told Swirl,

"Drop it, Mike, There's nowhere to go. Just put it down, man, it's okay."

However, this young white male in his fine clothes was in a state of shock, desperately needing a way out. Just then, Detective McAfee heard something coming from behind. He took a quick look: It was Detective Annie Potter; she was standing ten steps back and to the left of Detective McAfee with her gun aimed for Mike Swirl's head. Detective McAfee asked one more time,

"Put it down, man."

Mike then stopped all movement and said,

"I can't go to jail man,"

in a somewhat low voice.

I'm telling you man I can't do prison." Mike had had nightmare's of being locked away in prison half his young life.

McAfee stepped up one more step, just a little closer with his hand out, not quite sure what Mike was saying. Mike, still standing with a motionless body and holding the knife in an assault manner, began looking all about one last time Mike Swirl was still talking before he took a fatal jump at Detective McAfee with the knife! That is when Detective Annie Potter fired her gun, hitting Mike dead in the center of his forehead.

She continued walking, feeling bad about having to shoot Mike Swirl. As she reached the body on the ground, she heard Detective Rodney McAfee, who was now picking up the razor off the ground, say,

"I will never, ever understand what makes a man bring a knife to a gunfight."

Detective Rodney McAfee made two calls: one to Booker T., telling him to get a warrant to go though Mike Swirl's house and the other call went to the morgue.

Detective McAfee was there for the shooting. As head of the team answering only to the governor, no other calls were necessary. It took two hours for someone to pick up the body. While the two detectives waited for the morgue truck, they talked about going over to the Spot for some R and R.

A Night at The Bar

While he drove Detective Annie Potter to the Spot, he continued to assure her, *"Please do not feel bad. It was okay, the shoot was good!"*

Being in the Spot was like being in a sports bar. It was one huge area cut into two large rooms. One room had three billiard tables. In the other room contained small tables going along the walls. Each table sat two. Larger tables were on the inner floor. These tables sat four chairs. There were large TVs on every wall, in addition to three large-screen TVs on the wall behind a very long bar, adequately spaced apart. Rodney stood back looking at three bartenders who were two average-sized men, with one very sexy female working hard behind the counter.

Drinks were being prepared, they were mixing and serving as fast as they could. Their best was not enough on a busy night like tonight. Nonstop, they passed out beer in bottles and cans. The sound of glass tapping was loud as different colors of liquid passed up and down the counter. The two detectives, having worked their way in, felt lucky. This time of the night, the Spot was full of people who served and protected the law, along with one or two civilians, prosecutors, and public defenders. Some how he worked his way up to the bar while Detective Annie Potter went to find two seats. When he got the chance to order, he asked for "Four beers; call it a now-later – two for now and two for later."

More importantly, thank goodness, Annie had two seats for them. They had to share a table with two other people who looked to be deeply in love, whispering in each other's ears, giggling, and kissing all over each other. The two Detectives tried not to look at the lovers as they talked and drank beer for a while.

Their conversation was regarding the shooting of Mike Swirl. It was a good shoot; and she needed to believe it. After several beers, she started to feel a little better. She smiled as she looked around the room. Detective McAfee, looking at her face, knew it must be game time. Being one of the best arm wrestlers to enter the Spot Detective Annie Potter would put then down. She started with Detective McAfee and moved onto the next one in a long line, betting people twenty dollars a pop. O-yes twenty dollars lost or won

As she played for her rent, Detective McAfee thought more about the subject of Mike Swirl. He felt he could never tell Detective Annie Potter that the last words out Mike Swirl's mouth were, "*Kill me, bitch.*" Why did he feel the need to do what he did? Detective McAfee questioned to himself. That statement, "Kill me, bitch," tells me he wanted to go meet his maker. I can see that going away to prison, looking as good as he did, may possibly have been a predicament for him.

As Detective McAfee sat in subterranean thought, drinking his beer, he heard his name called out. *"Detective Rodney McAfee"*

He looked around and saw a face he had not seen for a long time: Detective Ben Sack, a man he had known from the armed forces in his younger years. They were both in the Navy Seals Special Forces for eight years. He was the man that Detective Rodney McAfee had written up for talking to Detective Gibson as if he was less than a dog. Detective Rodney McAfee was one of the captains of the team. Although they had been out of touch for some years, Detective Rodney McAfee invited Sack to join them.

As he introduced Ben to Detective Potter, he wondered, "What the hell could he want?" In addition, what happened to him?

The years had not been good to Ben Sack; his stomach looked to be nine mouths pregnant and growing. He was in a bad need of a shave, along with his salt-and-pepper hair receding. and Rodney began to talk a little about Ben and his life since the last time they saw each other. The conversation quickly moved on to Detective McAfee's life with much deeper questions. Detective McAfee felt the questions were excessively deeper and not about his life but about his work.

With questions like, "*What job are you working on now?*" "*Where is your offices located, McAfee?*" "*So who are you working with now?*" Ben know Rodney worked in secrete for people under the radar.

Detective McAfee had a lot to drink, but not enough to stop the discomfort from growing in his spine. Detective McAfee's discomfort said to him, "*It's time to go! Come on, Annie, we've got to go.*"

Detective McAfee made excuses as they walked out the door. While walking to the car, he could not shake the growing concern that their safety was in jeopardy. Detective McAfee pulled out from the curb, still not feeling right inside. Moving slow and thinking to himself about the case, he looked in the side mirror. A blue van started following them from one car back. Detective Annie having had too much to drink looked to be asleep already. When Detective McAfee's car turned, the van turned. The two detectives went to a hotel downtown to sleep off the beer. They checked into a room with double beds that allowed everyone to get comfortable. Detective McAfee slept until 8:25 a.m. When he awoke, he laid there thinking about last night. Then it hit him: the blue Ford van that was following them. He sat up looked at Detective Anne, who was sleeping sound in her bed on her back, with her mouth open and strange noises coming out of it. The covers had worked their way off, so Detective McAfee covered the woman he had come to love like a little sister and allowed her to keep sleeping.

Then he went over to the window, peeked out the corner while hiding behind the curtain so that he could see out, but no one would see him. "Darn-it," he thought. All he saw was the short roof of the hotel. This prompted Detective McAfee to go outside of the hotel. Once outside the front door of the hotel, he delightedly lit his cigarette. Then he walked over to the curbside, stood for a moment, and looked up and down the street. He saw the blue van. The hotel sat in the middle of the block, so Detective McAfee walked up to the corner. Once again, McAfee stood, looked, and puffed on his cigarette. He saw it, on the right side, three cars back from the corner. It was a blue Ford van with what appeared to have people sitting in the front seat. Detective McAfee could not see that Ben Sack and his helper sat in the blue van with orders to dispose of the Printer. They were fighting back sleep as they waited looking for Detective McAfee's car to pull out of the parking lot. While they sat, Ben Sack talked on and on about his hatred for Rodney McAfee and how his life went downhill after receiving that write-up. Because of McAfee, Ben Sack lost his stripes, busted down to private after having been in the service for seven years. 'After that I went to work for the Ohio Police Department working my way up to Detective but I got fired for not turning in all the money from some of the bigger drug busts I did, I decided to try my hand as a PI. Being a PI pays good money and my life is good now, working for this corrupt senator."

As Detective McAfee turned, he flicked the now-dead cigarette butt away out of his hand and then removed his cell phone from his front left hand pocket. He went to text messaging, and then pushed "Sent," which allowed him to view his recent text list. Detective McAfee clicked the button for J. Charley Woo and Gibson W. Goodwin; along with Booker T., He then inscribed this message that read:

"There is a bug on the wall!

"And my shoes are turning red!"

111

The team would know what it meant. "The bug on the wall;" Is their code for being watched. Red shoes signified dangers do not move. He then went back to the hotel. By this, time, Detective Annie was out of bed, wondering how she got there in the hotel. Detective McAfee told her about the blue van that was following them last night. He also told her of the great need to find a new base office to work in. If someone was onto McAfee and his team, they may be looking for the Printer to shut him up. Whatever the case might be, they could not lead them to the Printer. They checked out of the hotel. As McAfee drove, he did not see the blue Ford.

Annie asked, "Think we can go to my place to change my clothing? I smell like beer from last night."

"A quick stop will be okay," he responded.

Standing in the hall in front of Detective Annie's apartment door, McAfee picked up the newspaper from the floor and put it under his arm for reading later. Annie was in and out the bedroom smelling fresher than she did when she went in. The two detectives moved fast out the door and into the car. Breakfast was next on the list. As the two detectives rode around, Detective McAfee continued to look in the rear view mirror, out the back window for the blue van, but it was not there. The detectives had no time to waste; so as their food was being prepared, Detective McAfee pursued the newspaper for a new relocate for their base office.

He found one down on the Waterfront. It was a warehouse apartment, available immediately. "Call Oxford Realty 555-5555." McAfee made the call and set an appointment for 1:30 p.m. that afternoon. While eating at the diner, the two Detectives talked about the van and who might be the employer. Detective McAfee, along with Detective Annie Potter, returned to the car after enjoying their meal. While riding along Chestnut Street, a comfortable feeling came to them about the progress of this case. "The new base is the next stop" McAfee stated when he saw in the rearview mirror the blue van,

Detective Rodney calmly informed Annie who desperately tried to see it in the passenger mirror but could not. Detective McAfee went up two blocks turned his car onto Main Street and parked in front of an adult bookshop. Both Detectives stepped out of the car and went into the shop and held up their shields as they entered the front door. The employee quickly cleared a path for the officers who hastily walked to the back of the building, looking for the way out. There was an exit sign pointing the way out, but no door. Behind a stack of boxes was the back-door exit. Detectives McAfee and Annie stepped out into the alleyway and made their way out onto the street one block over from their car and the people who were in pursuit of them. Their escape onto the next street allowed both detectives to see the Super-Duper bus coming up, fast.

The Super-Duper Bus

The two detectives could not jump right onto the bus. Thirty or more people stood in line ahead of them at the bus stop. The detectives pushed, shoved, and worked their way up to the front of the line, pushing and stepping on toes as they boarded that bus. Detective Rodney McAfee first question asked.

"How much will it cost to ride this bus?"

The bus driver answered,

"Fare to ride this bus is five dollars, six dollars for transfers, and seven dollars to get a ride-all-day pass."

The gasoline shortage and lack of a gas keycard had made public transportation a grand thing today. Everyday more people were riding the bus as a means of transportation. In the early morning, people filled the sidewalk looking for a ride to work a retune home.

Columbus intersections throughout the city looks like a New York City street at noontime. The bus companies had to modify their buses to meet the demand of the public. The City council and the Mayor's office approved an emergency tax levy that hike the bus fare and replaced 75% of the bus fleet with the new Super-Duper Bus. Which was the use of two buses put together to make one long bus. Detective McAfee, thinking fast on his feet, got them on the bus. The money to pay for the ride was not in his brilliant plan. Detective McAfee had a ten-dollar bill, but no change. Annie walked past McAfee and took a seat in the back of the first half of the bus. Detective McAfee stood at the pay box behind the white line looking out at the people on the bus. It was heartbreaking to say, but all the people knew what he needed as he stood there, money in his hand.

The thought of using his shield for a free ride would not be right, but it was a thought. Now, most people knew that, if you did not plan to be involved, never make eye contact. Therefore, no one made eye contact with Detective McAfee as he looked out around the bus from face to face and asked aloud,

"Does someone have change for a ten?"

The people never did make eye contact with him as he held his money up in the air; he just could not obtain any help on the bus. Now the impolite bus driver stated aloud,

"Pay now or get off."

Then without having a drop of patience, he pulled over and said, *"You and your friend will have to get off, right now!"*

Detective McAfee looked at the driver with a hard look, the kind of look that said, *"Do you know who you are talking too, buddy?"*

The driver was being impatient and bold as he said,

"Well, get off."

The bus sat at the curbside with the door open, waiting for the two to depart. That was when Detective McAfee smiled at the man and said,

"I don't think so, sir."

Detective McAfee put away his money, and pulled out his shield, showed it to the driver, then he walked back to where Detective Anne Potter had sat down. He grew very angry at seeing the driver flying past a bus stop after the stop-requested point. The driver by no means gave the people time to get to their seats before taking off. Sending people flying into a seat was not funny. Some of the elderly people found themselves very embarrassed, already having a hard time boarding and sitting on the bus due to old age. The people paid the consequences for bad bus driver's mistakes. If only they had cars or gasoline for a car...

McAfee wished he could go up to the driver and smack him in the back of the head. How could he be so impolite to everyone. His face twisted up, showing his unhappiness for having to leave his own car and travel by bus. Now seated in an uncomfortable seat, The two Detective began spouting aloud about the things that are wrong with this buses.

Some may say the began to act childish but McAfee first commented

"These seats are so undersized that most people sit on top of each other as they travel to their destinations,"

"I know," replied Annie.

"They gave the new buses longer length, but what about making the seats wider too?"

Then McAfee went on to say, "*The actuality of the bus seating all the people that a driver will pack on a bus is awful, but when a driver over-packs a bus, one can't help but receive an ominous feeling. When you add that to the seats in the back of the buses that set so high up, a person's legs go to sleep from dangling down. If a need to move fast comes upon that person while their legs are sleeping that person will be in trouble.*"

Then other people joined in. A lady with short hair and glasses spoke up and said, "*How about the row seats? They are no better, being spaced so close together, your legs cramp up or your knees hurt.*"

Detective Annie Potter, as well as Detective McAfee, talked about the bus nonstop as they traveled across town.

"*Ring, ring, ring!*" It is the sound of a cell phone going off.

Everyone looked about to see who the owner was. A man in a blue, three-piece suit holding tight to a briefcase owned it. His conversation went like this: *"Hello? Hi, Dick how is every thing going? You need help. You ran out of gas at a closed-down gas station. That sucks. You stopped there because it is near to your house, only to find it shut down. Sorry, Dick, I cannot help. I am on the bus today. I have no gas in my car."*

After the man hung up his phone things went quiet on the bus for a short time, showing how bad everyone felt for Dick. Next Detective Rodney McAfee found himself working on the bus. The seat that flipped up and down remand up after a wheel chair, departed; causing a shortage of seats for other people The driver took what some would call forever to put the seat down, so Detective Rodney McAfee stepped into action to help. It was not his job to put that seat down, but he did. Detective Annie Potter found herself with an empty seat beside her while Rodney McAfee put down the flip-up seat.

The bus door opened for a younger woman, looking to be nineteen years old, to sit down beside Annie Potter. The younger woman was shaking, clearly upset as she sat there. Annie Potter, felt the girl's tension through her shaking body, asked in a low voice, *"Are you okay, sweetie? Is there something I can do to help?"*

The girl just stared down at the floor of the bus while her head moves side-to-side, saying,

"No."

Standing and holding onto the bar was a younger man with a backpack looking as if he was coming from school. He asked McAfee, "Tell me what you thank sir,

"If all the seats are taken, and standing up is a requirement to ride, should you pay full price?"

Detective Rodney McAfee never had the chance to answer, because a woman in front of them said, *"No, I don't, but what can we do?"*

She went on to say,

"I have a car but no gas in it. My gas day is on Saturday, and I always run out on Thursday night." The lady then states, *"One of the things I hate about the bus is the lack of cleanliness. At first look, things appear okay, but after you sit down, do not look behind the side seats or along the window tracks. Things you see could turn a stomach."*

Both detectives overly agreed with her as they all looked at the window tracks. The ride across town was long, with them stopping at every stop. The girl beside Annie began to cry in a low, muffled sound. Annie put her arm around her as she put a tissue in the girls hand to soak up some of the tears. She also gave a stronger request,

"Please let me help you, little one."

The girl stopped crying long enough to introduce herself. Jazmine Gordon was her name. Robert Gordon was her husband and they lived on the west side of town. Jazmine began to cry hard again, blowing her nose on the tissue her new friend had given her. Detective Annie Potter held her closer until she could talk again, that was when she shared, *"and I have to get some money together to get my husband out of jail. Robert had been grabbing old ladies' handbags to get money for our rent this month.*

He went to the corner store for bread this morning when an old lady riding inside a police car road past looking for the purse grabber. 'There he is,' she shouted, and pointed Robert out just as he entered the store. The driver pulled over, and both officers went into the store after him. With handcuffs placed on him, a black-and-white police car came with two more police officers to transport Robert downtown. Robert then called his friend's house next door to us, having them inform me where he is, and to help find a buyer for the gas keycards that Robert had in the top of closet."

Annie Potter asked the girl,

"Do you have the gas keycards on you now?"

Jazmine nodded her head yes. Detective Annie Potter then asked to see them.

Jazmine pulled them out of her back pocket and handed them to Annie. With the keycards in hand, Detective Annie Potter asked,

"How much are you asking for the keycards?"

Jazmine now had what was a large smile on her face. She thought about it, then said,

"One hundred dollars per gas keycard would be okay."

Detective Annie Potter went into her bag as if to get the money. Taking her time allowing Jasmine's smile to grow super large on her face.

Then is when Detective Annie Potter pulled out her shield, Jazmine Gordon expression quickly changed to a "I'm busted look." Detective Annie Potter had read a report on two young people earlier that day. The man got the gas keycards, and the girl sold them off. A black-and-white car was called to meet the bus at the next stop Officer Terry Spencer and Jazmine was taken away; if Jazmine was her true name off to jail she went.

The two detectives continued on their bus ride, which felt like it was forever when it was a forty-five minute ride. The things that Detective Rodney McAfee saw on this bus further sickened him in his spirit. Every part of him longed for a way to stop the shortage of gasoline so that everyone could go back to driving his or her own cars.

The detectives needed a new, unknown car, so when the bus went though the part of town that had automobiles for sale on every corner, the two detectives got off the bus.

Detective Annie Potter and Detective Rodney McAfee looked at cars, and then they looked at vans. They decided on a 2010 car with tinted-out glass windows. Sooner or later they will need to confront the people in the blue Van it just won't be today.

Gas Card/Roxanne Fredd

Back to the Governors office

Annie sat back in the new car, looking over her notes on the case while Detective McAfee stopped in to see Governor Andrew, giving impressive information on the conspiracy inside of the government, and how the Printer's information of a mob boss that led to the dirty Mayor Jones and a state senator. The plan was to have each one give up the other one, which is base Detective work. Too bad he did not have that senator's name as of now to strengthen this case.

The governor listened as he cleaned his fingernails, then he stated,

"This news comes as no surprise to me."

He continued to talk to his one-time good friend, Detective Rodney McAfee, saying,

"There are three words that I hold dear to me: "dictatorship, Equality, and Money." When money is involved, there is no equality. Moreover, dictatorship is not supposed to work in the U.S but it does."

Governor Andrew's voice began to rise, showing his distress as he went on saying,

"I know of several people in the government with a great fear of the gasoline running out; they have put together a plan to control the use of gasoline by the public. Nevertheless, the poor people are the ones getting hurt in this thing! It would have been great if the government had pronounce that they decided to spend X amount of money on vehicle-stop checkpoints, looking for people without a license and towing away their vehicle. That way, we can see who is still driving under suspended driver's licenses; the ones who never have taken the drivers' test at all, although they are out there, driving cars every day without insurance, and in that way the gasoline supplies may last longer."

He then asked Detective McAfee,

"Do you have car insurance?"

Detective Rodney McAfee nodded *yes.*

The governor continued his words,

"The rich people can afford to have specially made cars that run on things other than gasoline. These people are okay. Now that this gas keycard came out, it's middle-class people paying out the butt. They have both a license and insurance. The poor people missed this keycard deal. For one reason or another, they have no licenses, or they just cannot afford the gasoline. People are supposed to think the government is just cutting back, that way there will be plenty of gas for people that drive legally. However," Governor Andrew said angrily, pounding his fist on his desk, "It is about the damned money, plus control. The big wigs are trying to get rich off the poor people in the world, off the blue-collar man.

"I can see clearly how Dictatorship came out with a thing called mandatory gasoline keycards, after all! The government cannot just tell some people if you stop wasting gas riding around for fun, there will be plenty for the rest of us. Therefore, a law had to come forth that is stating 'you, and yes, you will not be driving today. These are the magical words that say we, as a people, are no longer equal at the gas pumps." Governor Andrew became overly sarcastic, moving him to a point where he started to laugh aloud. After a while he went on to say, "Your days of riding around, wasting gasoline for fun, are over, showings off those cars with the spinning rims. Only way to show them off now is by taking a photo, it will last longer."

Governor Andrew took a deep breath attempting to pull him-self together, then stated in a high-toned voice, *"Equality! How can that word have power when the new word is 'asked'? Where is your gas keycard? Did you say you do not have one? Then I'm sorry, but you can't have gasoline to use for your car.*

This kills that word 'equality at the gas pump.' "No license"! "No, gas keycard for you"! "No gas!"

Detective McAfee interrupted with a question, *"How can the government do something like this to the people and get away with it?"*

"Easy!" shouted the governor, growing upset again, *"Trust. The people trust their government, but not everyone is trustworthy. Some elected official are there for power and money not the people. With the government cutting people off from using gasoline, those people will not be able to drive."*

Governor Andrew, finding his funny side and his sarcasm, stated again, *"Ha! It's okay by me if those fancy cars with the loud music never, ever move again. The use of the loud tailpipes is over without a keycard! I stand with some of the other people in the government who feel these cars need to be off the road. The world of the loud music along with the jumping-up-and-down cars is over, without that keycard.*

"I ask you, Rodney, will this be dictatorship? If it is dictatorship, can it be acceptable in the U.S., today?"

Detective Rodney McAfee looked Governor Andrew in the face. *"How in the hell did a thing like this happen in the U.S., is a good question."*

Rodney up now out of his chair walking to the exit, when Governor Andrew said, *"Word of mouth from up on the hill is that there's plenty of gasoline stockpiled in bunkers across the U.S."*

Detective Rodney gave full attention to the words coming from Governor Andrew's last words,

"The best question for all of us would be how you, my good friend, and your detective team, are going to stop this thing from going on. We need to find out who is keeping the gasoline secret from the people in the U.S. Rodney, there is no shortage!"

At this point, Rodney stood with a deadly- game face

"I will find the truth and prove how this madness started." **After he stepped through and closed the door, Rodney McAfee paused on the other side to state in his low, deep, mannish voice,**

"I am not your friend."

The team did not know who was watching them. Thus, they needed to set up a new base. This time, the base office would be a large warehouse on the waterfront, with large bay lift doors. The team could drive their cars inside for cleaning and repairs on the bottom floor. The second floor was made of newly stained wood. It also came with a shower in the bathroom. All the same, equipment and beds now ordered for this office. Detective Rodney McAfee, called everyone to where he was standing

"Okay, people! First one on the list is the Big Boss man. Sometimes it is best to work from the bottom to the top, working our way up to the mayor and state senator"

Agent Flip of the FBI stood listening to the conversation with hopes of getting in on the fun. *"We need a surveillance team; Agent Flip you want a part in helping break this case open? Here you go. You and Detective Annie Potter will go in and place listening devices, plus cameras, on the front and back doors in the office and bedrooms plus the poolside at the Big Bossman's house. We will also need a diversion. That will be you, Detective Gibson. You will play the part of a drunk looking for his sister and pretending to call her on a cell phone repeatedly with a dying battery."*

"Detective Booker T has the construction floor plans for the building! Study it! We have no room for mistakes. We may have only one window of opportunity for this to work. Detective Booker T. also has a virus to put into the Mr. Big Bossmain computer. The problem is we must wait for Mr. Big Boss to go online. Until then, get prepared for the job."

There was nothing to do after getting ready for the job, but sit around looking at TV, playing cards, eating, and sleeping. Detective Booker T. and Angie had not walked away from their feelings for each other as they were told to do. They both felt even more strongly for each other. At night, Detective Booker T. would lie in bed, not able to sleep, feeling emptiness inside him; the deep longing to be with someone and that someone was Angie. He tossed and turned, wanting to go to her so he could hold and kiss her all night, but her safety had to come first. Often, while everyone else were fast asleep Detective Booker T. and Angie sat up on the phone all night, or until Angie's cell phone ran out of power. They talked of love, marriage, babies, and a house to live in, even the type of dog for the family. The name of the dog would be "Sniper." If Detective Rodney McAfee knew of this affair, Detective Booker T. would be off the case faster than a jet can fly. Therefore, he must never, know.

The Big Boss

The information from the Printer, Mr. Caskey, was a great help to the team. They established the name of Mr. Big, AKA Christopher Butler, who lived at 804 Willow Lane. The home was very large, the size of a small mansion, with servant quarters added onto the back of the house. He had five remaining people left in his service.

The taskforce team waited three days. Then, at 11:16 a.m., Mr. Big, AKA Christopher Butler, went online with his computer. This allowed Detective Booker T to release the virus he created specially for the job. Booker T. announced,

"With a push of this button, it is completed."

Then he stated,

"Now we wait for the boss to call a computer-repair shop for help."

The boss, very upset about the crash of his computer, grabbed a phonebook to find help. His telephone was tapped to intercept calls, and therefore, the first number he called, Detective Annie Potter answered, "Hello can I help you?" Then boss man questioned, *"Is this the computer repair shop on Morse Road?"* Detective Annie Potter replied 'Yes.' Happily, she set an appointment for the next day. The team had acquired the uniform for this job, just had to add the decals to them. Clipboard, in addition to paperwork will make it official.

The whole team sat around on that last free night, paying cards, a championship game of spades. *"The best two-out-of-three loser would pay for pizza tonight,"* stated Detective Booker T. Teaming up with Detective Woo, and Detective Annie teamed up with Detective Gibson. The game score stood even, at one to one. Detective Booker T. began to notice a look of discomfort on Detective Annie's face and asked, *"Are you feeling okay, Annie?"*

Detective Gibson joined in with true concern for Detective Annie's well being, saying, *"He's right, lady, you do look off point."*

Detective Annie than stated,

"Damn, you guys know me too well. It's just a little bit of pain in my foot. It's my baby toe. The nail has grown under and needs cut. The problem is, I just can't do pain and it will be more pain to dig it out but I must to get some freedom in the end."

Detective Woo laughed and said, *"I can take some pain, but Detective Rodney McAfee takes the prize for taking pain."* Detective Gibson agreed and stated, *"You're right. Do you guys remember the case we worked on not to long ago with the twin sisters? You know the one, where the one sister killed the other one and took her place to get all the money after their grandfather died. When Rodney McAfee came running around a corner of the back of the house in hot pursuit after the twin. Out of nowhere, she hit him! Smack! With the dirt shovel splitting a gash over his right eye.*

"The doctor put seven stitches inside and ten on the outside to close that cut, but the thing that got me was that he used no painkiller; that's right: without painkiller!"

Detective Woo, still laughing, said, *"Okay, but what about when he jumped up off the ground and started choking that cow? Her eyes were popping out of her head, and it took Gibson to take Rodney McAfee's hands off her neck."*

At that, time, the man him self walked up the steps to enquire, *"What's everyone laughing about?"*

Detective Woo gave an good answer.

"The past Rodney, we were just taking a look into the past."

Detective Rodney McAfee replied, *"Okay but the past is done. We must be prepared for tomorrow. I think you guys need to get to bed. Morning comes quick."*

The boss's home was like that of the rich and famous. Detective Annie Potter stood still on the marble floor, her eyes lighting up brightly. She began to describe the crystal chandelier in the large foyer to Booker T. through her two-way radio.

Detective Annie said,

"Man, I wish I could live like this one day!"

Then she remembered that she did not have the time to look at all the nice things The Boss had. While Detective Gibson played a drunk at the front gate. Annie ran around, placing devices, in addition to removing the viruses from the computer, All the people from inside the house went out side. They wanted to be of so helpful, calling his sister for him after helping charge up his battery some. It took everyone to handle him falling everywhere being a huge black man. By that, time Detective Gibson had calmed down from threatening to call the police if they did not let him in to see his sister.

Everyone agreed it's not a necessitate having the police stop by. Whenever Detective Gibson returned to the base, all the detectives had a good laugh at how helpful Mr. Big Boss's people were, trying to be so nice to Detective Gibson. Annie looked at McAfee and said, "Next, we infiltrate, right?"

McAfee nodded his head as he said, *"You're up next, Detective Woo!"*

Detective McAfee talked about how the rest of the game should play out. *"The Boss\ Mr. Big Bossmay need to replace our good friend, Mike Swirl. Therefore, you show up, looking for your friend, good old Mike. Say he told you to come by if you ever came to town."*

That night Annie had a hard time going to sleep in her own bed. Her head was full thinking of how beautiful a home Mr. Big Bosshad, with the marble floors going up the stairs and the plush carpet at the top. Your feet could get lost in it when you stepped onto the floor upstairs. The bedcovers were goose down, along with the pillows.

As she felt herself lying in the goose-down bed, she went off to sleep. Detective Annie Potter grew up in foster care. Both of her parents died in a car crash when she was seven. She went to live with her grandparents then, and her grandfather started touching her shortly after she moved in. By age nine, at night, her grandfather slept in the room with her every night, and her grandmother said nothing. One day, Annie went to school and told her teacher what type of life she had at home, and that she never wanted go home again. A call went out to protective services, which took Annie and placed her with another family. Living there, she never received new things. Secondhand was okay, because she had no one touching her at night. Sometimes Annie would sit all day, thinking of all the things she would have when she grew up, and most of the time it was things like Mr. Big Bosshad.

Detective Woo is ranging the doorbell at the Big Boss's house. That is prompting the house cleaner to answer the door. Detective Woo, is playing the part of Mike Swirl's best friend, who invited him to obtain a job working for Mr. Big. He asked the maid for Mike. So she showed him in to see The Boss. The two men talked for a long time about Mike and how good he was at getting girls in bed, and then dumping them. Detective Woo told of being in a competition with Mike Swirl at one time to see who could get the most girls. Going out and getting girls was one of the things Mike did for Mr. Big. It may have been Mr. Big boss's little head thinking, but the big head said,

"You have a job here!"

There was something about Woo that Mr. Big Boss liked, what that something was he could not at that time say. Now Woo's job was to go get girls along with obtain all the information he could on Mr. Big Boss.

Detective Woo stopped at the base after spending a week at the Boss's house. He had to give details to the team on the people who worked for Mr. Big Boss.

"There are six people including me living with Mr. Big boss: a maid to clean his home, a cook to prepare the food just as he likes it, a manservant to dress him, and the groundskeeper. The last on the list was the chauffer. They all live here in the servant's quarters. The servants are receiving extra pay for their extra ability. They are much more than the average servants are. They are skilled assassins, experts in their own field. Even though their pay was large, it was handed out quarterly."

Detective Woo continued as he poured himself a cup of coffee, "*The maid has a thumb ring with piano wire in it. She uses it to wrap around the neck, pulling until it decapitates the head, or she can use her hands to rip out the throat. The manservant has a hard head. When he hits your head with his head, your skull will open and your brains spill out as a cracked egg. The cook is the best with knives and cooks up a very good poison.*

Next is the groundskeeper, who is a gun expert. He can use any gun with precision. Last is the chauffeur. He has a black belt, and skilled in the art of pit-bull fighting style."

Detective McAfee said, "*All this protection around Mr. Christopher Butler? He should feel safe!*"

Detective Woo said, "*Yes, but he is so afraid of going to prison. He just hopes to get out of the game soon. His hands are too dirty with the gasoline hijacking and counterfeit gas cards, along with the dealing cocaine and heroin. He is really scared now that his main man, Mike Swirl, disappeared just like that.*" Detective McAfee said, "*Good Mr. Big Boss is shaken! Time is short. It is very important that we grab him , make a deal, and put him back in place. No one must know. The only way to trust him will be to take all his offshore bank accounts and shut them down so he has no escape money. The papers inside the safe should provide bank names.*" The surveillance team collected recordings, photos, dates, and times. They had info on money payoffs to members of the Columbus Police Forces currently working for Mr. Big Boss!

They located a safe built into the bedroom floor. The only one permitted in the bedroom was the maid, but the surveillance team had to see in the bedroom. Therefore, the team removed the portrait in the hallway drilled a hole through the wall, placed a small camera, there and then put the portrait back. Now surveillance could see into the bedroom. This gave them the number of the safe. However, Woo had one week to work the maid and get the key to go into the bedroom. He hoped to get the chance to make a print of the key with soft wax, but it was not easy. She kept the key on a chain around her neck, never taking it off. Each time he had sex with her, she would put him out of her room and lock the door behind him. Leaving Woo to return to his own room without the copy of the key .One day, he decided to put a little something extra in her drink.

"Okay, we have the key," reported Detective Woo to McAfee over the phone. Then Detective Woo got new orders, to make a cope of the personal effects inside the safe.

On that great day, the team would confront the Big boss; Detective Woo had the Big Boss riding with him, checking out Detective Woo's new car. It was a black-on-black Bentley Coupe, riding on twenties, plus tinted-out windows. Detective Woo and Big Boss had become very close, spending lots of time together, sharing secrets in the late night over a bottle of rum. The ride in the Bentley Coupe was the ride that would change the Mr. Big boss's life. This ride was fast, up and down the road, around the bend, ending inside of the warehouse office of the Gasoline Taskforce.

With guns pointed, the team yelled,

"Get out of the car, Christopher Butler." Detective Woo opened his own door to depart from the car. The Big Boss aka, Christopher Butler just sat there in disbelief. Detective Booker T, now laughing, shouted, *"Man, this is a photo moment."*

Finally, Christopher Butler removed himself from the automobile with an expression that was a mixture of pain and fear of prison on his face.

Detective Rodney McAfee asked, "*Do you want to talk?*"

All Christopher Butler, could do was nod his head.

Detective McAfee walked the man over to the table, sat down, and went over all the evidence they collected on him. "Unbelievable." The man began to cry saying, "*I was happier when I was just selling drugs. Nevertheless, you should know the mayor came to me with his proposition on the gasoline thing. The mayor called, talking to me of an unnamed senator who came to him with a get-rich plan. If I became part of their plan, things will be better off for me. Then the mayor told me how they would protect me. I believed him, because they are higher up on the ladder. Shit, look at me now.*"

Detective McAfee asked,

Will you help me get them?"

"Hell yes. I'll help you bring him down. Except I have one request, maybe I can get federal prison time. See I have never been to prison before, but I have been told by men that have gone in and out of prison that if a man hast to go, pray for Fed time because it is easer time"

All eyes went to Agent Flip, the FBI man. He shrugged his shoulders and said, *"I'll do what I can."*

Detective McAfee spoke up and said, *"Just so you know Christopher, You're offshore bank accounts have been placed under siege."* Detective Woo and Mr. Big Boss got back into Detective Woo's new car; their destination was Mr. Big boss's home. There are no words spoken between the two men. The Big Boss went straight to bed, with orders not to be disturbed. He stayed in his room, walking from wall to wall, thinking about what he could do and were he could run to hide with no money. He had some money put off to the side, but not enough to disappear. The Big Boss sat down on the bed, thinking about how to get out, but there was no way out. He has to stay and help the taskforce.

With everyone at the shop, Detective McAfee stood as the rest of the team sat, with full attention to the words coming from him. He has prepared a plan, to move in on Mayer Jones.

"Next step we need someone on the inside. Detective Annie Potter, you are up. It appears that Mayor Jones is in need of a new housekeeper. The current one has a sick mother, I believe, back in Cleveland, Ohio. Her good friend, Annie Potter, will stand in for her until she can return to work."

Going for the Mayor

Detective Annie entered the Jones house and started placing surveillance devices on the first day. Mayor Jones's home was nice but nothing like the Big Bosses home. Moving without restraint, she placed both cameras and listening devices in bedrooms and his home office, in addition to his car. Annie placed both a camera plus a listening device inside the Mayor's office at city hall. It would not be long before the taskforce would have all the evidence they needed to confront Mayor Jones.

Back at the base, the rest of the team passed time waiting for the next move. They still had five hundred gasoline keycard cards to retrieve. Detective Rodney McAfee had not forgotten.

The Printer, Mr. Caskey, gave them to Mike Swirl, who gave them to the big boss, and he gave them to an unimportant hoodlum called Little Black. After checking things out, Detective Gibson and Detective Woo reported at the base. Detective Gibson started out with,

"You're not going to believe this..." as he went into detail.

"I personally think a name like Little Black is very bold for a huge, white man."

Detective Woo jumped in and said,

Personally, I was looking for an African-American kid. However, it is an obese redneck man, the type I would give my candy bars to in prison; that way maybe I can escape getting hit and maybe losing more than just the candy."

Detective Gibson then jumped back in and said,

157

"This man has his operation set with ten large family vans that have fifty-gallon tanks. Fueling up at ten various gas stations, the vans receive their allowed amount of gasoline for the week. Then they return the vans to a closed-down lube station with a bay lift. The lift takes the vans up in the air; a man steps under the vehicle, removes the plug in the bottom of the gas tank, and drains out all the gas into a drum until a buyer comes. To purchase a drum of gasoline, a person will spend 25,000 for one drum."

Detective Woo, now in a hurry to put his two cents in, said,

"The money is split four ways: bottom man, Black, will keep two thousand; the Big boss, three thousand for him; Mayor Jones, ten thousand dollars; with ten thousand to the Senator."

Detective McAfee knew that once the money stopped coming in the mayor would know something was going down. He also felt in his gut that the mayor was set to run, because the Big Boss stopped calling so often. Detective Booker T. spoke up and said, *"From having looked over the surveillance on Mayor Jones, I can tell he is getting shaky and ready to run."*

Detective McAfee then said, *"It might be best to take the mayor at the same time as Black."*

Detectives Gibson and Woo moved in on Black with the help of the city taskforces. The two detectives sat in an unmarked car down the street until the *"go"* came from Detective McAfee. Detective Woo asked Gibson a riddle. *"If you had a five-pound bag of potatoes, how could you tell which one was the dirtiest one?"*

Detective Gibson, not being good with jokes, said, *"I do not know."*

Detective Woo said, *"You have to listen for the one shouting...*

Before he could give the punch line, Detective Rodney McAfee said, *"Move in"* over the car radio.

Detectives Gibson and Woo made the raid on Black's shop. The capture of Little Black and his twelve men would have gone smoothly with the help of the local police; however, there is always that one who thinks he can fight.

When the two detectives checked into the base, Detective Woo told everyone his story of how he checked in the bathroom for stragglers, and found one. The man must have had some hand-to-hand training, but it was not enough. Detective Woo blocked with a right, and the other moves were so fast. The man would never be able to say what happened, but when he woke up, he was in a hospital bed with a guard outside his door.

Everyone in attendance laughed for a short time, and then Detective Gibson announced he did take possession of the remaining gas keycards. When the "*Move-in*" call went out, Mayor Jones was in his office. Detective Annie pretending to be the housekeeper called him by cell phone from the parking garage underneath City Hall to be sure he was in. She requested a meeting with him in his office right now to talk about his house.

During their shared ride up on the elevator with other people, Detective McAfee whispered to his partner, "Man! There's something about that moment when the bad person knows the games over; the sad look on their mug, the moment we walk though the door. Having shield in hand, saying those magical words: 'You're under arrest.'" Detective McAfee walked though the door to the mayor's office first, shield in hand. Detective Annie followed. At that time, Mayor Jones requested a moment alone before Detective Rodney McAfee took him out of the office.

It did seem strange, but he was the mayor. The two detectives stepped out of the room, leaving the door ajar. Then Detective McAfee heard a load bang.

The mayor had attempted to take his own life. Detective McAfee called for help, and he traveled in the ambulance with Mayor Jones. As the ambulance traveled, an IV of saline was put into the Mayors arm to help replace some of the blood lost. His blood pressure was low, but steady. When the ambulance arrived at the hospital, the ambulance doors opened and a doctor-standing there to help the Mayor. He climbed on top of the gurney Mayor Jones was riding on. Next, he opened the mayor's shirt to expose his chest and began pushing on his chest repeatedly to keep his heart working as they rolled straight up to surgery.

After four hours, a doctor appeared to talk with the family Mayor Jones's eleven-year-old twin boys, along with the mayor's only sister, plus her husband. The doctor stated,

"We're not clear how much damage was done to the mayor's head. The bullet, a 22 caliber went straight through. He has some swelling to his face. He's resting in the ICU now. Now it will be about the waiting."

One twin began to cry uncontrollably from the report on his father, while the other one just rocked back and forth in his chair. The Mayor's sister tried to comfort the boys. She could not help but remember not long ago that these twin boys were here in this same room with their father praying for their mother's life to no avail. Detective Rodney McAfee overheard the sister and husband talking about Mayor Jones's living will that stops the use of machines to prolong life.

"Waiting is all we can do," were the sister's last words.

Detective McAfee ordered the team to do eight-hour shifts in Mayor Jones's room until a change came. The waiting went on for some weeks. The shooting was all over the TV news, in addition to the newspapers.

So I ask you, the reader, was the cat out the bag about the bust on Mayor Jones? The answer is no! Not if it was an attempt on the mayor's life, according to the report Detective McAfee gave to press.

"To the people of Columbus, Ohio, someone has made an attempt on Mayor Jones's life. If someone has information, please come forward to help."

"We must keep whatever we have on the mayor quiet," Detective McAfee told his team.

"If only we could get some of that Senator's information. Their name or gender, I am positive that this case will go downhill if the mayor passes away! Damn! Right now, we have nothing to go on."

In the beginning of the fifth week that Mayor Jones was in a coma, Agent Flip's job was on duty in the room keeping a watchful eye on the Mayor.

I'M IN LOVE

Sometimes, people can love too hard. The strong feelings that go with deep love bring on the need to tell someone about it. Detective Booker T had such a secret, even though the word *secret* means we can't or do not tell. He felt so happy he had to tell someone though. That someone happened to be Agent Flip. Detective Booker T talked on the subject of the strong feelings he had for Angie; how he longed to have a glimpse of her and hold her. He talked about the communications between the two of them every night. Being on a cell phone, they had to talk during the free minutes. Detective McAfee must never know he was still in touch with Angie. Then how their love had sense grown stronger for them, Detective Booker T. tells how desperately he feels. How he daydreams of holding her, and how, on some days, he cannot do his work because of it. Agent Flip devised a plan to cover for Detective Booker T. Agent Flip will cover his weekend shift.

That way, Detective Booker T. could spend Friday and Saturday night with Angie, and head back to work on Sunday night.

Detective Booker T. said,

"Great, it can work." On Friday, Detective Booker T. took off. On the way up the road, Detective Booker T. talked to Angie off and on, receiving directions on the way to go. Their time together was grand; they walked in the woods the first day, seeing all their eyes could take in. The wild woods gave them an enchanted feeling. Then at night, they laid in the yard next to each other so close; a bug could not get between them. There the two of them lie, looking out into the blackness of the night, lit only by the brightness of the stars. This felt heavenly to them both as they began making plans of an existence together. They promised each other a love that will last forever and a day. On the second day, they went back into the woods, walking and talking, until they came to a pond. There, Angie and Booker T. took off all they're clothing and jumped into the water.

As they played in the water, they became part of nature, enjoying each other in a way they had never enjoyed life or being with someone else before. Their spirit became as one from that moment on. When it was time to go home, Detective Booker T. said he hated his job and anything else that would take him away from her. He felt life without her life is not worth living. Leaving her was one of the hardest things Detective Booker T. had ever done in life.

Two weeks, had gone by before Angie thought about not getting her period for the month. She never said a word to Detective Booker T. or the Printer. This is her secret.

Detective Booker T. was on the road coming back to town. It was the end of the seventh week, and the mayor was still in a comatose state. Today, Detective Booker T. would return to relieve Agent Flip, who had sat all day on the job, guarding the Mayor. The hospital shift changed at 11 p.m., and the charge nurse for the Mayor truly has the hot for Agent Flip.

They would go into one of the rooms to make out often. Agent Flip passed his time away with the Mayor reading a book while the 3 to 11 nurse enters the mayor room. The time was 10:30 p.m. the last person on her chart before signing off work. Mayor Jones was still alive. Agent Flip decided now would be a good time to hold a pillow over the Mayor's face for as long as it would take to suffocate him. Smashing down on the Moyer Jones's face was out of the question. That will show there was a murder. A had a space of time allowing one half hour from 10:30 until 11:00 No one would ever know he did it. The 11:00 to 7:00 nurses came on duty to work. She never had a chance to check on the Mayor, who appeared to be alive. Being freshly dead, his color was still good. Soon as the nurse came into the Mayor's room, Agent Flip did as he always did grabbing her around her waist while he stepped close to her, saying, *"He's okay, come with me."* He was pulling on her as he was stepping backward out the room.

When he and the nurse returned from their hump party, the nurse saw that Mayor Jones's lips were purple, and his skin color had changed.

The nurse said, "*Oh, my God, he's dead*."

While she jumped into action, pushing the help button, Agent Flip stepped back up against the wall in shock and total disbelief. It looked like Agent Flip was working for the Senator from the start! That dirty dog was under deep cover, working for the corrupt Senator. Detective Rodney McAfee had sworn to the detective god that he would find that Senator's name and bring them down, along with all those working with them.

The team's work was at a standstill, due to the death of the Mayor. The detectives appeared to be stuck. The Mayor was the only one to talk face to face with this particular senator. They had to meet somewhere. Somehow, an exchange between the senator and the Mayor happened. The engraved plates that were used to make counterfeit gasoline keycard were of no help for fingerprints. The team spent great amounts of time thinking about a way to find out the senator's identity. Agent Flip went back to his FBI office to see what he could come up with there, although he continued to stop by every now and then, asking about Mr. Caskey and trying to get news of his whereabouts. Mr. Caskey was still his prisoner until his appearance in court. After a time, he stopped asking. Detective McAfee had assumed he let it go. Detective McAfee was on the case so deep he could not sleep. Some lawmen are born to be just that type. A diehard lawman, Detective McAfee is a lawman working inside the law; you really do not want him looking or thinking of a way to apprehend you, because, he will never, ever stop looking for his man.

The team has been looking at many different things when Detective Booker T. said, *"How about the surveillance tapes for the entrance at city hall? Everyone that would go in or out of the building should be on the tape for that day. If we crosscheck it with the sign-in book, we may have some luck. In addition, check all phone documents of the mayor's home, work, and cell phone."*

At last, the team began to feel they are going somewhere again. Their hard work of five weeks—looking at tapes and checking phone numbers—paid off. Detective Booker T. read the chart. *"There are two names that came up: Senator John Jamersion and Senator Rosanna T Tillman."*

Detective McAfee sighed. As he passed the photos of them around the room, he said, *"One of these two people may be the dirty Senator. Okay, now we need to look even deeper. You must go down into their past. Look under all rocks, big and small, to find whatever we can about their family and associates."*

Modern techniques are great things. If a person has some part of the story, he can get the rest. That is what Agent Flip did. He knew Detective Booker T. called Angie every night after seven. He used Detective Booker T.'s cell phone to track the signal, pinpointing a location for Angie. After getting the location of where Angie and Mr. Caskey are living, Agent Flip made his trip there, checking all around to see how the layout was set up, such as the woods and the cabin, Agent Flip made a plan for how he will kill everyone at the cabin soon.

On that day, Agent Flip decided to go hunting in the woods for the Printer, Detective McAfee decided to visit the cabin also. Here we have more of that great detective angel stuff.

When Detective McAfee arrived at the cabin, there was no one in sight. He looked out from the porch of the cabin. He could see no one, and then he heard the sound of two gunshots going off. He pulled out his gun while running in the direction of the noise. As he cut though the woods, he could hear yelling.

Detective McAfee could not tell who was yelling, but it was clear what they are saying: *Come on out. You can't hide.*

He worked his way around in the woods towards the sound until he came upon a scene that sent him straight into a rage. It was very hard to believe it was Agent Flip.

He had his gun out, pointed down at two people. The Printer and Angie on the ground, holding each other tighter than a knot in a rope, begging Agent Flip for their lives, but he responded, *"If it were up to me, I would let the two of you live up here forever, but my boss is having a fit about your big mouths."*

Detective McAfee aimed his gun at the back of Agent Flip's head. As he heard Agent Flip say, *"Sorry for your luck,"*

Detective McAfee fired his gun and hit Agent Flip in the head, clean through out the other side.

Detective Rodney McAfee then made two calls. This time, one went to the governor, telling him what he has done to Agent Flip of the FBI.

Detective McAfee alleged,

"The way I see it, this guy has been in on it from the start. He had no way to do away with these two at the FBI command center, so he turned them over to us, not knowing I would put them up in the cabin, way out of the way."

Detective McAfee talked for a long time about disposal of the body with the governor. The governor suggested putting Flip in the ground there in the woods to save a lot of paperwork on someone, not to mention an investigation into the death. Detective McAfee said,

"No, Agent Flip may be found one day, and it could be traced back to me at the cabin."

The governor then said,

"Go ahead, McAfee, do what you do. Whatever it is, I know it will be okay."

The three of them took turns dragging Flip's dead body back to the cabin. Next, they all split up to find Agent Flip's car. After it was located, Detective McAfee put Agent Flip in the front seat, on the passenger side. While Detective McAfee drove Flip's car, Mr. Caskey, the Printer, along with Angie, drove Detective McAfee's car. They went down the road for an hour or so away from the cabin, and then Detective McAfee stopped at a rest stop on the side of the road. Detective McAfee placed Flip in the driver's seat, took a rag, stuffed it in the car's gas tank, and lit it on fire. He walked to his car, got in the driver side, and pulled off. On the way back, Detective McAfee heard Angie talking to Detective Booker T. on the cell phone. He told her, *"Hang up, hang up, now."*

Then Detective McAfee took the phone and put it in his car's glove compartment. On the way back, Angie told Detective McAfee about Booker T. coming up to see her for two days, and how Agent Flip took Detective Booker's place at work so the two of them could be together. Angie also spoke of how deeply in love she and Booker T. had become, and of their plans to get married after the case is over. Talk of the baby never came up she felt the father Booker T. should be the second to know. She is the first to know of course. Detective McAfee headed back to the city after a quick stop at the cabin dropping off his passengers. He still has one more call to make, its to Detective Booker T. just to let him know how disappointment he was. He then had a long conversation with Booker T. about how not keeping an open channel almost got two people killed.

Booker's only reply to Detective Rodney McAfee was, *"If you had not forbidden us to be together in the first place, I would not have done things the way I did. However, you gave me an alternative. I could not make up my mind at that time. Give up Angie or be put off the case. I could not give up at that time. If you gave me an alternative now, I would say Angie, but I do apologize for deceiving you. It will never happen again."*

Detective Rodney McAfee then softened his tone as he said,

"I understand how it is when you're in love, but can you see? Two people almost lost their lives, and the death of Mayor Jones is questionable. Agent Flip had the last duty of overseeing the mayor on the night he passed away when it was your job to care for him. Look, I am not trying to point the finger at anyone. I just need everyone to stay honest and keep all the channels open, okay? Come on, let's go to work."

The Dirty Senator

Detective McAfee's first order of business at the base was to call a group meeting. All the detectives attended, looking over all the information gathered so far by the team. Detective McAfee talked about how Agent Flip was working for the other side. Then he had a long discussion of the feelings he felt about killing someone he believed to be a friend, stating,

"Agent Flip spent a lot of time with us, building up our trust. This was not the first time someone has let me down or portrayed the part of a friend, only to find out it was a lie, but I hope this is the last time for me. The cop in me feels bad about killing him even though he was a bad cop. It's okay if you all feel badly for Agent Flip being dead, but we can't become stuck there. It's time to move on to his boss, the senator."

Detective Booker T. sat in total disbelief about how underhanded Agent Flip was, plus he gave thanks to the detective gods for how grateful he was that Detective Rodney McAfee happened to go up to the cabin when he did.

180

Detective Rodney McAfee walked across the floor to the blackboards and asked the question,

"What do we have, people?"

Detective Booker T. walked over to the blackboard and placed his hand near the name Senator John Jamersion as he said,

"I had to look deep to get the information on this one. Old newspaper stories took me to some sealed records held by the CIA. Governor Andrew had to help us personally on this one, but I got all the details on the Senator and his family. First on the list is the Senator John Jamersion, born to Frank and Thelma Jamersion. On the day Johnnie came into this world, his family's last name changed to Jamersion. This gave little Johnnie an opportunity for a life free from the mob. However life still has a way of showing up somehow; at age thirteen, an attempt on little Johnnie's father's life opened the door of reality. The reality of who his old man is and what type of work his family did—the money laundering, gambling, and prostitution. The list goes on. Johnnie understood how his father was trying to keep him safe. Therefore, as John became a man, he looked on from afar with no hands in the family business. When John turned eighteen, he decided that the best way to have power in the U.S. is in government. After he graduated from college with a degree in government law, John got involved as a Notary Public, helping to feed the homeless and helping the community leaders while championing for

182

government jobs. John moved on to be a City Council member. From there, he moved on to U.S. Senator. His goal is to be president one day."

Detective Booker T. continued, *"Senator John has no senate aide, due to the premature death of the last one in a car accident."*

"Detective Gibson," *Detective McAfee called out, "you can fill that job as the senator's aide."*

Detective Gibson nodded his head.

Detective Booker T. continued, "*Next, we have Senator Rosanna T. Tillman. I had no trouble checking on her. She is public record. The people in her neighborhood spoke highly of her. She grew up on the east side of town in the low-income housing units of Columbus.*" *Booker T. stated as he cleared his throat, "There was only one parent in Rosanna's home, a mother named Vicky. She lived on crack cocaine for many years while on welfare, until Rosanna begged and pleaded with her mother to clean up. Vicky went to a live in drug treatment center in Columbus, Ohio, and today, Vicky has been living clean for eight years. She has a good job working for the state." Detective Booker T turned the page on his report and cleared his throat again. "One night, an attempt to rob Rosanna was made as she came home from work. She had no money, so the man sexually assaulted her in one of the abandoned building at age seventeen! Rosanna became upset with the law, because of how long it took the police officers to come to her area to take a report of the assault on her. The low-income housing part of town never received a quick response from the police. Rosanna felt the law was set up to work for some people and not others. Rosanna decided to get into government law to make a difference. She continued to work though her last year of high school. While Rosanna did this, she told everyone she spent time with her plans of getting into government law to make a difference. While attending college for law, Rosanna became city councilperson, than U.S. Senator. We might be able to put a secretary into her office."*

Detective Booker T. looked at everyone.

"Detective Annie Potter can take this job. Find whatever there is to find to help this case. Both of you detectives have four weeks, tops to get whatever there is to get."

In four weeks' time, Detective Gibson found out that although John Jamersion had friends in the mob, his hands were clean.

Detective Annie Potter became friends with Senator Rosanna's aide, Robert Stone, in two weeks' time. Detective Annie Potter took notice of how Robert Stone had mood swings off and on throughout the day. On the days that Senator Rosanna did not come into the office, Robert was able to keep a smile on his face. However, on the days Robert had to interact with the Senator, he went from happy to sad to morbidly unhappy. Detective Annie would say things to try to lift Robert's spirits. Sometimes it worked, but most times, it didn't. One day, Detective Annie asked, *"Robert, how about we go out for a drink."*

His reply was, *"Cool, why not?"*

They went to a quiet place the team had preset for taping. After one drink, Robert Stone was still sad! After two and three drinks, Detective Annie found a smile on Roberts's face. After seven drinks, Robert Stone was telling her all the business.

Detective Annie Potter began to see Roberts's fears of going to prison were real. *"The senator, she bitch has me do all the dirty work, acquiring the engraved plates for the keycards. She ordered me to acquire those plates! 'However you can do it, just do it! I do not care how! If you have to steal them, okay, but get them,'"* Robert said, mocking the senator's voice. *"Stealing is not for me, so I paid for you to get it done."* Robert then added *" It was not hard to set a workable price for the things she had me do . I also passed money to that private investigator guy that's always getting dirt on different congress people or supreme adjudicators to make them vote the way Senator Rosanna would have them vote. One of my side jobs for that senator bitch is money pickups or drop-offs that I turn over to her, excluding the money I take for myself from her. I don't see that as stealing. I call that my personal nest egg. I remember she had me set a dinner party for the CEOs of three large oil companies, where she played cat and mouse to see who would offer the highest pay for the guarantee of the approval of a pipeline going though an historic landmark.*

I have seen her do things you would not believe. Senator Rosanna has so many secrets she is keeping hidden from the public. Would you believe there are six silo bunkers full of tons of gasoline held there by Senator Rosanna and other members of the government, along with some defense officers?"

This was what Detective Annie Potter needed to hear. She asked, *"Are you sure about that?"*

"Oh, yes. That way, the prices for gas will keep going up." Robert began to sob tears about how sick and tired he was of that job. Then he spoke of knowing he could not get out of this without going to prison, since he was in so deep.

Robert Stone lowered his voice down to a soft whisper. As did this he rubbed his fingers over his nose simultaneously, blinking his eyes to fight back the tears. Then he said, *"I got a plan!"* Robert told Detective Annie, *"I will not go down alone. I have been keeping my own videotapes and files of Miss Lady, that senator bitch, ordering me to do her little get-togethers. I have numbers for all her secret offshore bank accounts. I'm the one that set them up in Rosanna's name for her, and she has two in her mother's name."*

Detective Annie Potter told Robert who she really was in a low voice up close to his ear: a part of the Gasoline Taskforce. At this time, Robert and Annie were truly enjoying the open confession about their true jobs. They had –no-way of knowing Senator Rosanna never ever trusted new people working around the office. The day Annie came to work at the senator's office, Rosanna had her private investigator watching Annie Potter's every move. He sat, hushed in close proximity, hearing bits and pieces of their conversation as they enjoyed their little party.

They talked on into the late night. The barmaid gave last call for alcohol, although it would not be their last drink of the night. The private investigator moved out to his car to call Senator Rosanna, telling her of the conversation he took secret tapings and other possessions he held. The investigator received orders to continue watching the two people, until they split up, to dispose of them and get those belongings The next stop for the two over-intoxicated people was Roberts's house, a one-level ranch style. Robert removed one of his hard wood floorboard from his living room floor then gave Detective Annie all the stuff he had stashed, with hopes that it would put Senator Rosanna away for a long time. Detective Annie Potter had two last drinks with Robert, and then she set out for home. She had had too much to drink to drive across town to the base.

A quick look at the clock told her it was too late for her to have called someone for help. Being the big girl she was she felt she could handle it. There were two things all detectives on the team must have at their homes: a hiding place only McAfee and Booker T would know about, the second was a hidden motion sensor camera so everyone would know what happened if or when one of the team happened to fall fatally. There would be no rock large enough to hide under for the killers.

The medicine cabinet in the bathroom was the place Detective Annie used to hide things. It came off the wall when you pulled the whole thing straight out, showing the two-by-fours in the wall. Detective Annie was drunk, but she followed protocol, she put away the evidence and went to bed. Having had too much to drink, she never heard the door open as the killer let himself into Annie's apartment. She never felt her killer standing over her bed, as she laid in it, asleep. He slowly took the pillow from under her head. Detective Annie's head turned to where the light from the bathroom glowed on her sweet face.

As he looked at Detective Annie's face, he thought to him self, "*I know her from somewhere.*"

Nevertheless, that would not stop the killer from doing his job. He held the pillow in his left hand, and the thought came again,

"*Where do I know this lady from?*"

He placed the pillow lightly to her face. He put his gun with a silencer screwed to it on the pillow and fired three times into Detective Annie's face though the pillow. Then he searched all over the apartment for the papers and tapes that he never found.

Unfulfilled in his search and very tired, he left Annie's place, heading to his car. Then out of nowhere, it came to him just who she was: Detective Annie Potter, Detective Rodney McAfee's girl! His steps slowed down. It was as if the knowledge of who she was started his whole body to freeze with fear. The gunman went to his car and just sat, gripping tightly to the steering wheel, saying, ""*#, #, #, what the # will I do now! I know Detective McAfee will be coming for me, #!*" He continued to sit and stare blankly up Summit Street, and then his last thought on the killing of Annie was, "*Oh, well, can't cry over spilled milk, time to move on.*"

From there he went to the home of Senator Rosanna's aide, Robert, and did the same thing to him, after which he tore apart the house, looking for the things that were no longer there. Feeling tired and overworked, the killer found himself driving down Parsons Avenue. This murdering night appeared to be extremely long. He stopped at a red light long enough to see the all-night store open for business. When the light turned green, he pulled into the parking lot and went into the store, right to the alcohol section of the store. His hand reached for the MD 20/20, a wine that might or might not help the feeling of fear that had control of his gut. He opened the bottle and put it up to his nose. The whiff brought a smile to his face as the bottle moved down to his mouth. Swallowing nice and slow the taste felt great going down. The killer sat, sipping and thinking of different encounters he had in the past with Detective McAfee some good and some bad. In between that, the sweet face of Detective Annie Potter would jump out at him in his mind, like how the light from the bathroom put a glow on it.

Before long, the bottle of MD was gone, so out of the car and back into the store he went. This time he purchased two bottles of MD 20/20 and returned to his car. There he drank, and in between drinking, he wished he had some of that great stuff that made Detective Rodney McAfee the man that he was: full of integrity and love from so many people.

A phone began to ring, bringing about a rise from the gunman. It was morning. He had fallen into a deep sleep, dead to the world in his car at the store parking lot. On the phone was Senator Rosanna, checking to see if all her orders were or had been carried out? The response she received was "No" to the retrieval, and "Yes" to the disposal. This did not make her happy. She just happened to be out of town, but retuned shortly after the story broke over the news about the two murders of two people from her office killed.

The rest of the team went off the deep end with sorrow over Detective Annie's death. They gave themselves time to grieve in their own way. Detective McAfee took a fifth of gin home, with orders not to be disturbed. Detective Booker T went up to the cabin. After he got there, he was surprised to see that Angie had put on a lot of weight. He could see that a baby was coming. Together, they decided if it were a girl, her name would be Annie. Booker T.'s heart still was in pain while he was there. Detective Gibson stayed at the office, struck with disbelief. Detective Woo went home to see his family.

They all had two days to cope as best they could, and then get back to the office.

"Two days was not long enough, but it will have to do. It's time to close this case," McAfee shouted with an angry tone in his voice. "It's been almost one year. Let's put it to bed now."

While the team went through the death of their good friend, Annie, Senator Rosanna T. Tillman became even more desperate, and as time went on, her desperation cultivated into raw fear. Finding the things her aid Robert had on her became the most important thing in her life. She told the killers

"Do whatever it takes to get those papers or make them disappear! If you cannot do it, say so I can get someone else to acquire the papers and do away with them."

She could not take the thought of everyone finding out how dirty she was. Her life as she knew it would be over.

Detective McAfee, Gibson, and Booker T. walked down the hall in Detective Annie's apartment building. The door to Detective Annie's apartment stood left slightly cracked open. Everyone stopped, and with one motion, all unsnapped and took out their guns. Detective McAfee pushed the door open slowly, looking in with his gun pointed up at the ceiling. What they saw was breathtaking. Detective Annie Potter's apartment looked desecrated. Her sofa and loveseat cut up, with padding everywhere. The TV was on the floor. Bookshelves turned over, with books all over the floor. They walked on into the middle of the room and could see Detective Annie's bloody bed cut up and flipped over onto the floor. Detective McAfee just stood there, stunned. Detective Gibson continued to check though the place for an intruder. Detective Booker T. walked on to the bathroom, which was located to the right of the bedroom, with his gun pulled out, ready to fire. He removed the medicine cabinet and retrieved the recorded DVD of Detective Annie's killer and the information on the senator. No one said a word until

Detective Booker T. came back from the bathroom and said, *"Let's go."*

All three detectives walked out the apartment door, putting away their guns, and headed to the car. They got in the car without saying a word. Detective Booker T. got halfway down the block, when there was a large booming sound behind them. It was powerful enough to shake their car. Detective Booker's foot hit the brakes, and everyone jumped out of the car and stared down the street. The thing they saw was just what Detective McAfee needed to wake him up. There was an explosion. The blast was strong enough to blow down Annie's apartment building. Smoke and fire was going up into the air. They heard the sounds of fire trucks and rescue vehicles going there, in the hopes of saving just one person.

Detective McAfee loudly said, "Get in the car." The street was full of onlookers standing outside of their cars, coming out of their houses, and getting off the buses.

The street quickly became full. Detective Booker T. made his way around them, blowing his horn in an attempt to get their attention as he drove around them all. Silence came back into the car, not out of grief, but out of gratitude. The detective angels were there with them.

Detective McAfee spoke up loud and clear: *"From here on, everyone sleeps at the base in shifts."*

Detective Booker T. drove, while Detective McAfee looked over some of the papers on the senator. There was crucial information there. Detective Gibson just sat still, looking out into space. His mind went back to when he was over in Vietnam on his first run. A woman was standing outside a burning hut, crying for someone to help her. Detective Gibson did not understand fully, but he know someone inside the fire needed help. He took a blanket, doused it well with water, covered his head with it, and ran in, only to come out with a baby that looked to be fifteen months old.

As soon as they entered the base, Detective McAfee put in the DVD of Detective Annie's killing. While they all watched, a powerless feeling came over each one of the detectives.   Their feelings then changed from anger to rage, and their eyes filled up with tears from the love for their coworker. Each one had to turn their head and walked away slowly, except for Detective McAfee. He looked at the man he had been close to at one time: Detective Ben. McAfee's mind went to the night he and Detective Annie were out drinking at the Spot. Detective Ben came in with all his questions about Detective McAfee and the team. He introduced Detective Annie to him that very night. Detective McAfee full of rage went over to the table, took out his gun, and started cleaning it. As he did so, he shouts, "Let's get some rest. It will be a long day tomorrow. Booker T, before you go to bed, I need you to take the offshore bank accounts of Senator Rosanna and donate all that money to wherever it is needed in the U.S."

The team may have laid their bodies down for the night, but no one could get right to sleep. The scene of Detective Annie's murder was stuck in their heads. Detective Rodney McAfee could not sleep, either. All he had in his head was facing Senator Rosanna Tillman. He set up on the side of the bed and replaced his shoes. From the bed, he walked over to the desk then grabbed up a portable DVD player with the copy of the recorded disc of the murder. He also took with him a copy of a tape, the one of Robert, the Senator's aide, telling secrets to Detective Annie. Detective Rodney McAfee traveled over to Senator Rosanna's home. It was late, so he knew she would be home. At her door, he knocked hard with his fist. There was no immediate answer, therefore, his knocks grew longer and harder and louder. After a time, the door opened. The she-bitch herself stood there in front of Detective Rodney McAfee, wearing a long, thick robe, fit for a queen. Being full of rage, Detective Rodney McAfee did not wait for the appropriate *"Can I help you?"* or *"Come in, please."* He just pushed his way in. He looked all around at the nicest things money could buy. He started to talk, *"My name's Rodney McAfee,*

Detective Rodney McAfee, appointed by the governor himself. My job, as head detective of the Gasoline Taskforce was to put a stop to you getting rich on the pain of the people. I took this job to stop the illegal printing of gasoline keycards, and I found out where the two tanker-trucks of gasoline could be, with hope of retrieving the gasoline. I never thought I would be in the middle of a government conspiracy! We had no way of knowing where these things would stop. In 2004, people accepted the gas hike to support the fight in the Middle East. Time went on, the price went up, and people began to question why they were paying such high prices for gasoline. After the conflict in the Middle East ended, gasoline should have gone down, but it didn't. Now we know why, People with greed and power could not stop hungering for the money they made. This conspiracy is like a virus spreading though the government. The year is 2024 now, and my team and I are bringing it down. I may not stop it forever, but this part of the virus, with you in it, will die."

As he talked, he saw the senator looking with a very smug look on her face; the look that says, *"You can't touch me!"*

This was the look she had as she looked at the large, priceless artwork on her wall. This look continued until Detective Rodney McAfee turned on the recording of Robert her aid talking. He could hear a bone pop in her neck as her head snapped around, looking for where the sound was coming from. Senator Rosanna did not dare to look Detective McAfee in his face now. He never really know why he had to come here to see Senator Rosanna. Although at that moment, badass Senator Rosanna had that look on her face; you know, that look the same look Mr. Big had, sitting in the car at the Taskforce's office, and the same look the mayor had before he put that gun to his head. Now Senator Rosanna had it, too. In addition, let us not forget about the girl, Jazmine, on the Super-Duper Bus. Detective McAfee loaded the DVD player with a copy of Detective Annie's murder and set it on the end table. As it played, he walked out the Senator's door.

Standing, astounded by the info Detective McAfee had left behind, Rosanna did not know what to do. Her door stood open, allowing the cold chill of the night to return Rosanna back to her senses. She walked over, slammed the door shut with her foot and then she ran up to her bedroom, took out a suitcase, and began to pack. When that one became full, she pulled out another. Before long, she had five bags packed. Her next thought is where to go. Rosanna hand reached out to for the phone. She felt the need to call a travel agent, only to put the phone back down.

Whispering to her self *"No need to panic, I can drive myself out of town until morning and stop at a bank to get some money. I can transfer it from one of my offshore accounts,"* she said to herself.

Back at the base office, Detective McAfee sat up in his car until he passed out, still sitting behind the wheel. Today everyone is dragging about, with their heads hung down, still feeling the pain of Detective Annie's death. Everyone sat in what was supposed to be a circle, holding a cup of coffee in hand. Head Detective McAfee, Detective Woo, and Detective Gibson all sat down as Detective Booker T had the floor.

"What do we know?

"We have the tapes and DVDs from Annie's house. We have a name for the scum who killed her: Ben Sack, a hit man working for the senator. His address may vary from place to place, but we will find him. We also have the things Annie got on the senator. I will make copies to send out to all news stations, along with the governor."

"I say we just kill her," announced Detective Woo.

Detective McAfee said, *"No! We are all hurt about Annie, but we must stay within the guidelines of the law, or we would be no better than them."*

McAfee then stated,

"I feel this will hurt Senator Rosanna all the same. We have the places she has stockpiled gasoline, along with Senator Rosanna's other helpers, like other U.S. Senators and congress members on the take, as well as Supreme Court judges. If we do it this way, we will help the people and put Rosanna away forever. Booker T, you continue making copies to send out. Detective Woo, you stay here and help hold down the fort. Detective Gibson, we have a man to go and see about a dog."

Detective Gibson, having worked years with his friend, knew this meant they were going to check around the base for trouble, then go looking for Detective Ben Sack. As Detective McAfee's car pulled off, he saw the blue van down the road sitting still so he just rode around the corner and parked. He knew if the gunman,

Detective Ben, was watching them from the van, he would be close enough to see them leave the base, and he would try to get those papers back. Detective McAfee and Detective Gibson got out of the car and walked back to the base. As they came though the alleyway, he and Detective Gibson heard guns firing.

Using caution, they came up to the door with their guns out. Detective Gibson stood behind McAfee, trying to see what was going on. Detective McAfee ducked his head around the door one or two times and after bobbing in and out; he saw two sets of people shooting at each other. His men were on one side, pinned down by gunfire. There were five men, Ben Sack with four other men, who had automatic guns. Detectives McAfee and Gibson entered the warehouse, firing their guns, joining in the firefight against Ben Sack and his men. Detective Gibson shouted, *"I am hit in the arm!"* McAfee shouted, *"Booker T, go ahead send the files out over the computer!"*

Detective Booker T worked his way to the computer to hit the send button while shooting his gun off. His hand was on top of the send button when the power went out.

Ben Sack was firing his gun when he saw the power boxes on the wall where he was standing. It took no effort to put his hand out, and he pulled the switch down as he said, *"I couldn't let you do that, Rodney."*

McAfee, now more upset as if that were possible, shouted back, *"Ben, good buddy, some things you just can't stop."*

At that moment, the back-up generator jumped in to play. Booker T hit send. There happened to be only one way out, and Detective McAfee stood there at that door. The guns continued to fire. When it ended, there were three men killed. Ben Sack was one of them. He would be going down to the morgue. The other two gave up. They would be going to prison.

Detective Booker T having had already transferred all of her offshore bank money to different places, which left him, feeling good about helping needy people in the world. He also sent out more emails to the CIA, news stations, the FBI, and the U.S. President.

While this case appeared to be over at this point, the gasoline shortage was still a part of life. Mr. Big got his wish: he would be doing federal time. The mandate still in effect, stops those people who did not have license from driving, even when the gasoline supplies began overflowing. The team would be continuing onto the next job.

However, this case was not over for Detective Rodney McAfee. After packing her car, she drove herself to the town of Pittsburgh. There, she made attempt after attempt to get money transferred, but there was no money. The news about Senator Rosanna's work on Capital Hill could not found her.

Senator Rosanna went on the run. hiding down in the black swamp water of Louisiana with a cousin. After two years of crocodiles and mosquitoes, she decided to come out of hiding, cutting her hair short and dyeing it platinum. She changed her name to Jacqueline Bean, and moved to the small town of Tupelo, Mississippi. She had lived there for six mouths, and she was starting to feel that life was good. There, she made a move on a young pastor in need of a wife. Rosanna felt that being a pastor's wife just might fill that emptiness deep inside of her: the longing for power and control she used to have as a senator.

One day, she attended the evening revival at her church. While sitting down in front, she felt someone tapping on her shoulder. She looked back, and there sat Detective Rodney McAfee, holding his shield up to her face as he whispered, *"Damn there's that look again,"*

Now that this case was over, Detective Rodney McAfee could rest, but he would never, forget his good friend, Detective Annie Potter.

See you all on my next case.

The End

McAfee – Detective Rodney McAfee

Al ways at the service of the U.S. Government

Rodney McAfee continued to enjoy the night air. Sitting back on his cabin porch, he felt the lateness of the night; that prompted him to look down at his watch. The time was 10:30 p.m. "Good time for me too go to bed." he thought.

Rising from his chair, he put out his arms to stretch, while he took in a deep breath of night air. All in one motion his steps taken to go inside the cabin door. He went straight to the shower and onto bed. Sleep came quick for Rodney McAfee, but it did not last very long. The time was 2:30 a.m., Rodney McAfee was jumping up out of his bed. The pounding on the front door was nonstop! Someone on the other side needed inside badly! Rodney was out of bed in a daze. He's desperately looking for his left house shoe! As he looked for it, he shouted the words, *"There better be a good reason for this!"*

The president needs help, and she needs it fast. Rodney began to give his full attention to the words coming out of the president's mouth.

"Rodney, if I may call you that, I have checked, and you seem to be the man I need on my side at this time."

Rodney had taken a position over in the corner of this office. Which allowed a good view of the whole room, as the president began to talk about the problem at hand. Rodney listened, but he could not stop himself from looking back over where he entered this room. He could not believe the craftsmanship that went into the sliding bookcase he had entered this room through. It filled the wall, top to bottom. A person would never think a secret elevator exit was there.

The case of

The Five-Million-Dollar Horse

Made in the USA
Charleston, SC
14 July 2011